CHANGE OF HEART

By K.M.Neuhold

CONTENTS

SYNOPSIS

Does my husband's heart still miss me now that it beats in the chest of another man?

Lub-dub
A heartbeat more familiar than Easton's own

Lub-dub
He vowed to love his husband until death do they part. And then the worst happened.

Lub-dub
His heart kept another man alive. River. A stranger in the world with Easton's husband's heart pumping the blood that warms his skin. Does his heart ever miss Easton without knowing why?

Lub-dub
Sweet, kind, beautiful, River. Easton never meant to meet him...never meant to know him...never meant to fall for him.

Lub-dub
Easton loved River's heart long before he ever met him, but is it possible he's falling in love with his mind and soul too?

***Change of Heart is a stand alone story

with strong hurt/comfort themes, mild bisexual awakening themes, and a HEA

COPYRIGHT

Book and Cover design by Natasha Snow Designs
Editor: Editing by Rebecca

PROLOGUE

Easton

I'm numb from head to toe. I can see the doctor's lips moving, but I can hardly hear what she's saying over my pulse thundering in my ears. This can't be happening. There's been a mistake. *Not Paul, anyone but Paul.*

"Mr. Harrison?" The doctor says, reaching out to touch my arm. I can see her hand as it rests on my forearm, but all I can do is stare at it, unfeeling. This must be a nightmare.

"I'm sorry, what?" I ask in a stupor, waiting to wake up safe and sound in bed beside my husband, burrow into his arms, and tell him about the *horrible* nightmare I'm having.

"I know this is difficult, but he's lost all brain function. He's being kept alive right now by machines. For all intents and purposes, he's dead," she explains for the second time, and bits of the conversation come back to me now.

"And you want me to pull the plug so you can give his heart to someone else," I recall what she already told me.

Her smile is apologetic and reassuring, I'm sure she's a good doctor, but I fucking hate her.

"He's an organ donor," she hedges, clearly implying this is what Paul would've wanted if he could make the choice for himself.

It's too much to think about right now, too big of a decision to make. How can I know what Paul would want? I mean, fuck, he'd *probably* want to have not gotten hit in the head so badly on the job site that he ended up brain dead. He'd *probably* want to be on his way home to argue with me over what we're going to have for dinner before kissing me silly and agreeing to whatever I want.

I can't breathe.

Dragging desperate breaths in and out of my lungs, my head is swimming, my vision going blurry from the tears spilling over.

"I don't know. I don't know."

"I know this is difficult," the doctor says again. "If time wasn't of the essence for this other patient, I wouldn't even be asking you this so soon, but your husband is a perfect match, and if we don't get this patient a heart soon, he's going to die."

This man I don't know, have never met and never will, is going to die just like Paul is dead. Right now, I don't think I could give less of a fuck if every person on the planet were to drop dead if it somehow meant I could have my husband back. But there's a rational part of my brain still functioning that reasons keeping Paul artificially alive a few more days won't bring him back, but it just might kill this other man. This other man who probably has people who love him as much as I love Paul.

"Fine," I agree through a choked sob.

"Mr. Harrison, you have no idea how much this will mean to him. I'm sure it's what your husband would have wanted."

I nod, starting to grow numb again. How can any of this be real? All I keep thinking of is Paul's arms around me eight hours earlier, the soft kiss he pressed to my earlobe while I filled his travel mug with coffee. He'd whispered, *"You're the best thing that's ever happened to me,"* just like he'd done every morning for the past five years, and I'd laughed and pushed him away, rolling my eyes at how cheesy he was, even though we both knew I loved every second of it.

Why hadn't I said it back? Why didn't I wrap myself around him and beg him to stay home today, safe and sound in bed? Why did the kindest, most gentle man I've ever met have to be taken away from me when we've barely even started our lives together?

I reach down and run my finger over the smooth metal of my wedding band on my left ring finger, easily remembering the bright smile he wore on our wedding day. I thought we were too young to get married, thought it was a bit heteronormative, couldn't understand why it meant so damned much to Paul, but I loved him, so I agreed to do it anyway.

Another sob wracks my body, and I wish

like hell it was me in there instead of Paul. How am I going to live without him? How am I going to go on without the absolute love of my life by my side?

CHAPTER 1

5 Years Later

River

The sun shines brightly through my office window, beckoning me away from my computer and out into the world. It's the first warm day of spring, making it all the more difficult to stay chained to my desk rather than going outside to feel the sun on my skin and drink in the smell of spring as it makes its first valiant attempt to vanquish winter. I want to take my Tablet out to the park to sit on a bench and draw. I want to get out of this damn office.

Nice days like today have a way of making me a little melancholy in a strange way. Of all the days you'll live, so few of them will be this perfect. Most of them will be too hot, too cold, too rainy, too snowy. These days are too fleeting, and before you know it, it'll be gone, and that's one less perfect day left in your lifetime.

I laugh and shake my head at myself, turning back to my computer. God, I'm being morose today. Maybe I really should get out to stretch my legs for a little while or risk the next ad campaign I put together channeling my inner Good Charlotte.

Standing up from my desk, I stretch my neck and then my back, lifting my arms over my head to help work out the kinks in my shoulders. Picking up my phone, I text my best friend and co-worker, Brandon, to see if he's up for grabbing a cup of coffee with me. Well, if decaf can even be considered coffee. After having to outgrow my caffeine addiction overnight after my heart transplant, I could take or leave the decaf crap. But coffee is so much a part of the corporate ritual, if I don't pretend, I feel like a bit of an outcast. If you don't need smoking or coffee breaks, is there even a socially acceptable reason to leave your office?

Brandon appears at my door looking as over today as I feel.

"I was two seconds from texting you the same thing. I need to get out of here for a few minutes before I go postal."

"We can't have that." I pat him on the shoulder and give him a friendly push in the direction of the elevators.

Brandon and I met back in college. Freshman year, we had dorm rooms directly across the hall from each other and discovered we had a lot in common, including both planning to work toward an MBA in marketing. The next year we decided to look for an apartment together, and the rest is pretty much history.

When I ended up in the hospital the year after we graduated, he was right there by my side, playing card games with me and watching shitty daytime TV while we waited to hear if I'd get a donor heart in time.

I knew the odds of getting a match before it was too late were slim to none. With over one hundred thousand people on the transplant list, only about two percent get a heart. I looked it up. There wasn't much else to do while I was laying in the hospital bed waiting to die.

It was surreal. I'd walked into the hospital with Strep Throat, and it looked more than likely I would leave in a body bag.

I was only twenty-five, and neither of us knew how to process it. My mom visited every day and cried over my bed as if it was already a casket, but Brandon always managed to bring things back around to being more bearable with his careful avoidance of the elephant in the room.

When the doctor came in to tell me they found me a heart and we were going to surgery, I couldn't believe it.

I could've died; I nearly did.

As we wait for the elevator, I reach up and put a hand over the scar on my chest. I can feel it through my button up shirt, rough and huge.

And after all that, here I am, spending my afternoons staring out the fifth-floor window of my office, pretending to work. There has to be more to life than this, doesn't there? Not that I hate my job; in fact, I mostly love it. I wanted to work in marketing, and now here I am at a successful firm, making a good living. But it feels like something's missing. It feels like there should be more.

"Everything okay?" Brandon asks, noticing my hand on my chest.

"All good, just in my head too much today."

"How about we go out after work?" he suggests, and my enthusiasm for the idea is underwhelming. I don't drink, don't eat most of the shit they serve at bars. I never say no to a round of pool, but I'm starting to feel like I'm living *Groundhog Day*, doing the same shit over and over.

"Meh," I reply with a shrug.

"Meh? What's the deal?"

"I'm not in the mood to play pool and watch you flirt with twenty-one-year-old women."

"Last time I checked, you love twenty-one-year-old women," he points out.

He's not wrong. I do. But lately, even bringing a beautiful woman home feels empty and boring. It would be easy to chalk it up to the fact that I'm thirty and might be ready to find someone special to settle down with, but it's not like I haven't tried that. I've had a few serious girlfriends over the past five years, one of them I even considered proposing to. But the feeling of something missing always got to me in the end. None of them seemed to ever chase away the bone deep loneliness that settled over me the minute I woke up from my surgery. It felt like I was missing part of myself. I've heard of amputees having phantom limb syndrome, can you have that with a heart? Because that's what it felt like, a hollow, gasping need in the center of my chest that no one I'd met had been able to soothe.

Don't get me wrong, they were amazing women, and I was lucky to even get the time of day from them, I just couldn't get over this feeling like there was something *more* I was supposed to feel. Or maybe I've bought into the Hollywood bullshit too much, and the whole idea of someone who makes your heart race and turns your life upside down is just a fairytale.

Easton

With the end of a gray colored pencil between my teeth, I stare down at the panel I've been working on and consider the expression on the hero's face.

Reaching for my favorite mug sitting beside me, smelling of lovely chai tea, I pluck the pencil from my mouth and trade it for a sip of tea. I hold the mug in front of me, looking at it as if I haven't memorized every inch of it a thousand times over —the chip on the rim just over the handle, the faded image of one of my first characters drawn on the front with a silly caption. It was Paul's favorite mug. I got it for him for our first wedding anniversary, and he refused to drink out of anything else. He said one day that mug would be worth millions.

My chest aches with a familiar longing. You'd think after five years it would be easier to think of him, but here I am with a lump in my throat and new cracks forming in my heart at the sight of his damn mug.

I set my tea down and push my papers away, getting up from my desk to stretch my legs. I'm way ahead of schedule anyway; a little break won't hurt anything. Not that getting behind schedule would be a huge issue either. My graphic novels sell so well, my publisher bends over backward to kiss my ass.

Another pang starts in my chest. No one believed in me more than Paul did, but I didn't land my agent until the year after he died. He never got to see the success he was such a huge part of.

Apparently, this is going to be one of *those* days where Paul's ghost haunts every single one of my thoughts. Some days I hardly think of him at all, and then I realize I haven't thought of him all day and feel sick with guilt. I know it's not how he would want me to feel, but no matter what I do, I can't let go of all the what-ifs and wishful thinking.

I wander into the spare bedroom where all of Paul's things are packed into boxes. After all this time, that's as far as I've gotten. Packing it all up was hard enough—I can't imagine getting rid of any of it. Not that it's making me feel much better to let it gather dust in the bedroom that should be my studio but instead is a mausoleum for memories.

Reaching into the nearest box, I pull out the note he wrote to me and pinned to my refrigerator after our first hookup.

East,

I'm not sneaking out and blowing you off. I have to get to work, and you looked too cute sleeping to wake you up for a proper goodbye.

Last night was the best night of my life, and if you don't call me, you can bet your ass I'll be turning up on your doorstep to make sure I get a date.

Xoxoxo,
Paul

I run my fingers over the words, feeling the indentations from the pen strokes. His handwriting is messy and nearly illegible. I would give just about anything in the world for one of his sloppily scribbled grocery lists that left me squinting at the paper in the middle of the cereal aisle trying to figure out what the hell *onurdes* were.

My throat is thick and aching with unshed tears as I reach into the box again to see what other treasures I can find hastily stuffed inside.

It takes me several seconds to recognize the card I pull out next. It's a fancy Thank You card with watercolor flowers on the front. When I open it, a gasp falls from my lips. I forgot this card even existed. When it came from the hospital, I glanced at it and hastily stuffed it away because it was too hard to read.

Now, I take in the neat penmanship, loopy letters carefully scrawled as if each word was painstakingly considered before being written.

When the hospital offered to deliver a thank you note from me, I wasn't sure what I would even write. I'm still not sure, clearly. I didn't know if getting a thank you note would make things easier or more difficult for you. I don't know anything about you other than that you had to give someone up so I could live, and for that, there aren't enough words to express my gratitude.

I may not know your name or anything about you, but I will always owe my life to you and your husband.

Thank you from the bottom of my heart,
River Williams

Tears stream down my face unrestrained as I read the words a few times over, trying to feel grateful that there was some shred of good in Paul's death. But I don't know this man. He's carrying a piece of Paul through the world, and for all I know he could be a murderer, someone who wears socks with sandals, or someone who says *supposebly* instead of *supposedly*. He has Paul with him everywhere he goes, and he could be anyone.

This isn't the first time this thought has occurred to me over the years. I've lost track of the number of strangers I've passed on the street and wondered if they might be the person with my husband's heart beating in their chest. Would I know if I saw him? Would some part of my soul recognize the little piece of Paul living on through this man if I spotted him in the grocery store or a coffee shop?

My phone vibrates in my pocket, and I consider ignoring it, but if it's Fox, he'll chew me out for not answering.

Pulling my phone out of my pocket, Paul's best friend's face fills the screen, so I swipe to answer.

"Hey, Fox," I answer, sounding every bit as morose as I feel.

"Everything okay, East?"

I sniffle and wipe the back of my hand across my damp cheeks, tossing the card back into the box where I pulled it out from.

"Oh yeah, these are happy tears," I say sarcastically.

Fox is quiet on the other side of the phone for so many heartbeats I consider just hanging up on him. I would if I couldn't clearly picture Paul telling me to be nice to his best friend. I'm sure he's trying to figure out what to say. For the first few years, we would do the "Do you want to talk about it" dance when he would catch me breaking down, but it's grown old, and I think he's trying to find a gentle way of telling me it's time to get the fuck over it already. I know what he'll say without him needing to say it—*Paul would want you to be happy. Paul wouldn't have wanted your life to end when his did. Paul wouldn't want to see you closing yourself off from everyone and still crying over him in the middle of the afternoon five years later.* I know because I've said all these things to myself over and over until they've lost all meaning. The words are just incomprehensible sounds to my ears.

I'm sure there are a lot of things Paul would've wanted for me, but I don't know how to do any of those things. How do I move on when the love of my life is gone? How am I supposed to feel happy when Paul *was* my happiness? How am I supposed to stop crying when all the color is gone from the world without Paul here? *Paul* isn't the ghost—*I am*.

"What can I do?" Fox finally asks, sounding strained and tired. I have no doubt he sees it as his duty to Paul to make sure I'm okay, to take care of me in the way Paul would've wanted.

My gaze flickers to the box again, and an idea starts to form in my mind. I don't know why, but I need to know what he's like, this man whose heart is the same heart I memorized the beat of a lifetime ago. Does his heart ever miss me without him even knowing why?

"What would you say if I asked you to track someone down for me?"

Fox joined the police academy out of high school, but after taking a rogue bullet to the shoulder, he retired after only five years. He moped around for a while, living off the benefits he got for being injured in the line of duty. Until he decided to start up a business as a private investigator. From what Paul said, he's damn good at it too.

"Who do you want me to track down?" he asks cautiously.

"River Williams."

I hear rustling and then the scratch of pen against paper. "Who is this guy? That's a unique name so that should help, but I'm going to need a little more to go on than this."

"He had a heart transplant five years ago."

The writing stops and Fox sighs. "East…"

"Please," I say, clutching my phone tighter in my hand. "I just…I need to know." I sniffle and I'm ashamed of how pathetic I sound, but it's nothing worse than what Fox has heard from me before. This is the man who held me countless nights and let me cry all over his shirt, the man who always had soothing words for me even when I couldn't stand to hear them. I know he would do anything for me…for Paul…and if I have to push him to make this happen, I'm shameless enough to do it.

He sighs again, this time sounding resigned. "What do you need to know?"

"That he's a good person, that he's… worthy."

He lets out a humorless laugh. "It's a little late if he's not. What are you going to do if he turns out to be a prick? Cut his heart out?"

"Please?" I say again.

"If I do this, you need to do something for me."

I hesitate, already sure I'll hate whatever he's going to ask for. But now that the idea of knowing about this man has come into my mind, it feels vital in some way.

"Fine, what do you need me to do?" I agree.

"I need you to *try*. Go on a date, hell, go out with friends, get out of the house and do something fun."

Even though I knew it was what he would ask, the demand sounds entirely unreasonable. But if I want him to find this River Williams, I know I have to agree.

"Fine."

CHAPTER 2

River

I lift a glass of ice water to my lips and take a sip, my eyes scanning the bar out of habit more than interest. Brandon is chatting up a couple of cute women, every so often giving me a subtle head nod in an attempt to encourage me to come join him. I can practically hear him in my head telling me he's got them on the hook, and I should come join him because there's more than enough to go around. As if he won't happily take them both home for a night of fun once he gives up on me taking one off his hands.

"Designated driver?" A sweet feminine voice says from beside me. I turn to find a petite redhead wearing a low-cut green shirt and a pair of jeans that may as well be painted on. She's gorgeous, exactly my type, but I can't summon the required enthusiasm to do much but nod.

"Always," I answer vaguely.

"That's nice of you." She takes my half-hearted answer as an invitation to sit down, sliding onto the stool next to me and angling her body toward me. "I'm Victoria."

"It's nice to meet you, Victoria. I'm going to

be honest. You seem lovely, but I'm not looking to take anyone home tonight."

Her shoulders slump a little and she sighs. "Figures."

"I'd be happy to buy you a drink though," I offer, and she perks back up.

"Deal."

I wave down the bartender, and Victoria gets a drink.

"So, do you have a girlfriend or is it personal?" she asks once she has a beer in her hand.

I consider lying and saying yes just to spare her feelings, but decide she seems too sweet to outright lie to. "No girlfriend, but it's not personal. My head's been in a weird place lately; I'm no good as far as company goes."

We chat for a few minutes before I politely beg off, standing up and tossing some extra bills on the bar for a tip and then waving at Brandon to let him know I'm heading out. He shoots me one last look, and I shake my head and offer him an apologetic smile before slipping out the door.

The cool night air wraps around me, the din of the bar fading as soon as the door closes behind me, leaving only the scattered sound of cars passing and the occasional drunken laugh escaping into the night. An overwhelming emotional exhaustion hits me, and the task of walking the half-block to my car seems insurmountable. I lean against the rough brick outside of the bar and tilt my head back, looking up at the expansive night sky. The light illuminating the bar entrance flickers, and I close my eyes as an inescapable feeling of loneliness hits me square in the chest and nearly brings me to my knees. I drag in a harsh breath, putting a hand over my heart, and wonder for the millionth time about my heart donor. Did he love someone so much he could hardly breathe? Is there someone out there still who loved him the same?

I drag my fingers to the center of my chest, tracing the raised edges of my scar through the soft fabric of my shirt. I can feel the beat, steady and even against my palm, and I think about the man who saved my life. I don't know a damn thing about him, but that doesn't stop me from wondering who he was, what kind of a life he lived, who loved him but selflessly made the sacrifice to save the life of a complete stranger?

A clicking sound echoes in the night; it sounds like a camera. I open my eyes and look around, spotting a man across the street with a camera. I furrow my brow, squinting into the darkness to get a better look at him. He looks familiar, but I don't think I know him. Have I seen him somewhere before?

I don't have long to ponder it before he gets into a car and drives off.

With a heavy sigh, I push myself off the wall and start for my car, my emotions seeming to tail along behind me like a cape, heavy on my shoulders. It's horrible to say, but sometimes I wonder if there was someone more worthy of this heart than I am. Did someone die because I was one spot further up the list than they were? Was a funeral held for someone who, if they'd gotten this heart, would've gone on to vaccinate sick kids in Africa, or argued to overturn wrongful convictions for death row inmates, or, at the very least, someone who left a family to mourn them? Not that my mother wouldn't have been sad if I'd died in that hospital bed, but she would've gotten over it.

I wonder, for the millionth time, about the person who's lying in an empty bed mourning the loss of their husband whose heart now pumps blood through my veins. Would they think I'm worthy of his heart? Am I?

Easton

Two weeks after my request for information on River Williams and I'm sliding into a booth opposite Fox at his favorite pub downtown.

"Hey, East," he greets me, leaning over the table to kiss my cheek.

I spot the folder on the table in front of him, and I'm so anxious to see what's inside, I nearly snatch it to see for myself. But my fear of what might be inside stops me. I wanted to know who River was, but Fox's words are ringing in my ears now. What if he is a prick? Or worse, what if he's a criminal or all-around bad guy? Do they give heart transplants to criminals? They must, right? If he *is* a bad guy, there's nothing I can do about it. I could be stuck with the knowledge that Paul's heart is beating in the chest of a domestic terrorist with no recourse.

"Take a breath; it's good news," he assures me, putting a hand over mine.

"It is?" I suck in a lungful of air and hold it for a few seconds before slowly letting it out.

"He's a good guy—works at an advertising firm downtown, donates to NPR, recycles."

Relief whooshes through me, and then all of his words start to register. "He works downtown? As in, he lives *here*?"

I don't know why but I'd been imagining him living somewhere far away.

Fox narrows his eyes at me, using his free hand to pull his folder closer.

"You got the information you asked for, now you have to uphold your end of the bargain."

"What? Wait, you have to know more than that."

"What more do you need to know?" There's a sort of pleading in his eyes. He wants me to drop it, to move on. I would if I could.

"What does he look like?"

"Why does that matter?"

"I don't know," I snap. "I don't know why any of this matters, but it does. I can't stop thinking about it. Maybe if I can put a face to this man, I can finally move on."

"Honestly, I don't see what good knowing what he looks like would do. I don't see how any of this will help."

"Please, Fox?" I beg, my voice quivering. "I don't see how it will help either; I just need to know."

He takes his hand off mine and opens the folder, pulling out a photo and passing it over to me. I'm not sure what I was expecting, but he looks like an average thirty-something man—dark hair and eyes, light stubble on a square jaw, a slight bump on the bridge of his nose that suggests a break at some point, a smile on his lips as he talks to whoever he's with. Don't get me wrong, he's attractive, but I was expecting...I don't know what I was expecting actually. I take a few seconds to study the rest of the picture. He's entering Cool Beans, a popular coffee shop downtown, wearing a nice suit and accompanied by another man—a friend? A lover? A co-worker? Who knows.

"Are you satisfied now?" Fox asks gently.

I shrug, feeling numb all over. "Not really."

He gently takes the picture back from me, puts it back into the folder, and slides the folder off the table, tucking it away somewhere unseen.

"So, how's the new book coming?" he asks, deftly changing the subject as I flag down the waitress for a drink.

"Almost finished."

"Nice. Is it in color like your old ones or still black and white?"

"Black and white." I don't tell him I can't find joy in colors the way I used to. I can't find joy in anything, and I *know* this isn't the life Paul would've wanted for me, but he's not here so what the fuck am I supposed to do?

CHAPTER 3

Easton

I woke up craving coffee. It's all I've been able to think about all morning as I finished up the final few panels of my graphic novel. I don't keep coffee in the house, generally preferring tea. But today I want coffee...from Cool Beans.

It's not about River Williams. I have no reason to even think he'll be there. So what if he was there in the photo Fox took? Maybe it's the only time he's ever been there. No, it's not about River—it's about coffee.

After making several copies of my finished novel and stashing them in various places, including one in the safe in my bedroom closet. I take the copy for my publisher and put it into an envelope to take downtown so I can drop it off.

I'm never too careful, always hand delivering the final manuscript myself. It's a beautiful day, perfect for a long walk and a stop for coffee on the way home.

My agent, Mark, is thrilled when I show up with my manuscript in hand. He gushes for a little while about my sales and how happy the publisher is, and I nod politely, making my escape as soon as socially acceptable.

My heart beats faster as I near the coffee shop. It's silly; he won't be there. And even if he *is* there, I won't talk to him. What would I even say? *Excuse me but you've got my husband's heart.*

I shouldn't go. Fox said it himself: no good can come from this weird obsession I'm developing. It's probably time I call my therapist again and set up time to talk. I went to see Sheila regularly for the first few years, but eventually it started to feel pointless, talking about the same thing week after week and not getting anywhere. So, I stopped going, promising her I'd save her number and call if I needed to talk. She stressed that grieving a loss like this takes time and can come in waves. This sudden need to know about the man with Paul's heart is just another wave, and it will pass like all the others have. In a few weeks I won't care about this man; I'll be back in my cocoon of numbness. A small vacation into insanity might be the most excitement I have all year. I might as well roll with it.

Cool Beans comes into view, and my heart jumps into my throat. I shove my trembling hands into my pockets and quicken my pace, my eyes scanning each passing face, *not* looking for River.

And then I see him. I didn't expect I actually would, but there he is, only a few feet away, made of flesh and bone, Paul's heart beating in his chest. He's real and so close I can almost reach out to touch him. For a second, I can't breathe, I can't think, I can't do anything but stare at him.

Just like in the photo, he's wearing a nice suit, navy blue with a light blue collared shirt, no tie. He's looking down at his phone with the ghost of a smile on his lips, the afternoon sun caressing his hair, showing highlights of auburn among the several shades of brown. The stubble on his cheeks is thicker than it was in the photo; he probably hasn't shaved since it was taken.

He's beautiful if I'm being honest, but what hits me more than anything else is that if I could feel the heat of his skin, I would know it's warmed by the blood pumped by Paul's heart.

It happens so fast. He's looking at his phone while his feet continue to carry him forward as if on autopilot. He doesn't see the bus barreling closer as his foot leaves the curb.

"No!" The word tears from my throat, and people around me stop to look. I shove past them, blind to anything but River and the bus. I've never moved so fast in my life, the panic turning me into something superhuman.

He doesn't look up until my hand wraps around his upper arm, and I yank him backward, just as the bus whizzes past, the driver laying on the horn as the gust of wind from it ruffles through our hair.

River

"Holy shit," I gasp.

My heart thunders erratically in my chest,

too hard and too fast. I can't believe I was nearly flattened by a bus. I can't believe I was stupid enough to step into the street with my nose buried in my phone. I can't believe this man saved my life. This man who's still gripping my upper arm hard enough to bruise and looking at me with blind panic and relief.

"It's okay, that wasn't my first near death experience," I joke, trying to ease his worry, even while my own hands are still shaking from the rush of adrenaline. "I'm kind of glad you were here to save my life though."

"You're welcome." He finally lets go of my arm, giving me a sheepish smile before looking away.

My heart gives a strange flip in my chest, probably still from the recent shot of adrenaline as I look at the man. There's something that feels oddly familiar about him, and I study his features trying to place him. But I'm almost certain I've never seen him before. I feel like I would've remembered his delicate features and sweet smile. His hair is a mess of brown curls, his eyes deep pools of blue, like the calmest part of the ocean. There's a blush spreading over his cheeks, and I wonder what he's feeling so shy about. He just saved my life; he's joined my personal list of heroes right next to the guy who gave me his heart.

His eyes flicker over the rest of me quickly, and it's hard to tell if he's checking to make sure I'm okay or if...he couldn't be checking me out, could he?

The thought heats the pit of my stomach. He's definitely cute, and what a *how we met* story this would be. But before I can even follow that train of thought, my usual nerves kick in, twisting my stomach in knots at the thought of making a move on him.

He gives me another quick smile before stepping back out of my personal space, and I'm immediately hit with the urge to follow him, to not lose the contact so quickly.

"Can I buy you lunch?" I ask, as much to my surprise as it is his. His eyes widen, and he darts a glance around like he's afraid he's about to get caught for something. My hand drops to his hand, and I notice a silver wedding band on his left ring finger. My heart sinks a little, even if it *is* for the best that he's not available. "You know, as a thank you for saving my life," I continue so he doesn't think I'm asking him on a date.

"You don't have to." With his right hand, he twists the ring around, not meeting my eyes.

"Come on, I hate eating alone," I cajole.

"I guess it couldn't hurt," he agrees, biting his bottom lip and running a hand through the messy curls atop his head.

Putting my phone into my pocket before it nearly gets me killed again, I check for the walk signal and then usher the man across the street.

"I'm sorry, I didn't catch your name," I say.

"Easton."

"I'm River," I introduce myself, offering my hand as we walk. He takes it, and his skin feels smooth and warm against mine, oddly inviting. A flash of his warm hands running up my arms and over my chest has goosebumps forming on my flesh.

I shake off the thought, stopping when we reach my favorite cafe at the end of the block.

"What?" I ask, noticing the strange way he's looking at me, like he can't decide if he wants to laugh or cry. "Is something wrong?"

"No, it's just...my husband loved this place."

Okay, so maybe he *was* checking me out. I didn't miss the past tense either. But he *is* still wearing the ring.

"He passed away?" I guess gently.

"Five years ago."

"I'm so sorry."

Easton gives me a tight smile. "Me too."

Once we're seated and our orders are placed, an awkward silence descends between us. I'm not sure why I had the impulse to invite a perfect stranger to join me for lunch, even if he *did* just save me from becoming roadkill. God, Brandon would've been so pissed if after all this I died because I was too busy looking at Facebook instead of where I was walking.

"So..." I say, taking a quick sip of my water to wet my dry tongue. "What do you do?"

"Aside from saving strangers from stepping in front of buses?" he jokes, the hint of a smile forming on his lips. It's not a full smile, but it makes me curious, makes me want to find a way to bring out a full smile to see what it looks like on his pink lips.

"Yes, aside from that," I agree with a chuckle.

"I'm an author. I write graphic novels."

My eyes go wide and a giddy, fanboy smile spreads across my face. "Holy shit, you're not Easton *Harrison*?"

A blush pinks his cheeks, and he dips his head, reaching for his own glass of water and avoiding my gaze, even though I can see the smile widen a fraction.

"That's me," he confirms.

"This is crazy. I love your novels. I think I've read *Hotel Nowhere* at least a dozen times."

His blush deepens. "Thank you."

"Can I ask you a question?"

"I'm not giving away any spoilers," he warns, finally looking back up at me with pride and embarrassment in his gray-blue eyes.

"No, nothing like that. I was curious why your first two graphic novels were in color while all the rest have been black and white? There are so many theories about what it's supposed to symbolize, and some of them make sense, but sometimes I think we're all reading too much into it, and it's just a stylistic choice? Or hell, maybe you ran out of colored pencils and didn't want to buy any more."

K.M. Neuhold

The light in his eyes dims, and he reaches for his water again, this time taking several sips, his Adam's apple bobbing with each one, before setting it down and reaching for his napkin. He balls it in one fist, his gaze fixed on the table.

"Sorry, should I not have asked that? Fuck, can we forget I brought it up?"

"No, it's just..." He blows out a long breath and looks up at me again. A single tear leaks from the corner of one eye and rolls down his cheek. He doesn't bother to wipe it away, just lets it fall. "I wrote and drew the first two before Paul..."

Oh. "Paul was your husband."

"Yes. Since he's been gone, it feels like all the colors are gone too. Nothing's the same without him."

His words and the emotion behind them hit me in the chest like a sledgehammer. Just when I've been starting to doubt the existence of can't-live-without-you love, Easton blows my world apart. My heart starts beating faster again, and I want to reach out and touch him, find a way to comfort him, ask what it's like to love someone that much. Except, I'm sure for him it's horrible. He had a soulmate, and he's gone.

"I'm so sorry," I say for the second time, even though the words are woefully inadequate. Reaching out, I place my hand over his, and his breath catches, a hum of electricity or connection or...I don't know what, goes through me, and somehow, touching this man I've never met, this man who saved my life, feels like the most important thing I've ever done.

The waitress chooses that moment to appear with our food, shattering the fragile moment into a million pieces at our feet. I pull my hand back and give her a tight smile.

"I need to go wash my hands; I'll be right back," I tell Easton, pushing back from the table and heading into the bathroom.

I'm sure it looks to Easton like I'm fleeing from the uncomfortable moment, and maybe I am a *little*, but I do actually need to wash my hands before I eat. The anti-rejection meds I have to take for the rest of my life mean that my immune system kind of sucks and getting sick would be *very* bad.

I take my time washing my hands, using my elbow to get paper towel out of the dispenser and then using that paper towel to grab the door handle on my way out of the bathroom.

"Sorry about that," I say when I get back to the table. "I had a heart transplant five years ago, and I have to be really careful about...well, just about everything—hygiene, diet, exercise."

Something flickers across Easton's expression too quickly to decipher.

"Wow, that must be difficult to deal with."

I shrug and pick up my fork to spear a leaf of lettuce from my salad. "At least I'm alive."

Sadness passes over his expression again, and I wince at my words, feeling like a complete ass.

"Shit, I didn't mean—"

"No." He holds a hand up and gives me a half-smile. "I'm..." He clears his throat. "I'm glad you're alive too."

It's a strange thing to say, but weirdly comforting. This whole interaction with this strange man has been every level of weird and confusing I can imagine, but I don't regret inviting him to lunch. There's an odd sort of comfort in his presence. It's like I know him, even though I don't.

We eat in silence for a few moments, letting the serious mood hovering over us settle. With each bite of lettuce I chew a thought starts to occur to me. It's a crazy thought, a pointless thought, an embarrassing thought. But how many chances will I have in life to meet and talk to an artist like Easton? If I pass this up just because it's awkward, I'll be kicking myself later.

"I've actually been working on a graphic novel myself," I blurt before I can talk myself out of it.

His eyes light up, and he leans forward with interest, the entire mood shifting between us. "Oh yeah?"

"Yeah, it's not very good. I do digital drawing, and I'm still getting the hang of it, and the story is kind of juvenile."

"You should see my early, unpublished stuff; it's embarrassingly bad."

"I doubt that."

"Oh, trust me. I have them in boxes at home. You should see them; you'd laugh your ass off."

"If you're offering," I half-joke. I'd cream my fanboy jeans to get a look at those.

Easton blushes again, taking a big bite of his sandwich and chewing slowly before shrugging. "Sure, why not? If you want, you could bring some of your work over too, and I could maybe give you some quick critique or pointers."

"Are you serious?" My voice borders on giddy. "That would be...Holy shit...I mean, that would be *incredible*."

"No big deal. You can come by this weekend. We can order takeout and talk shop," he offers.

Fanboy down.

"Yes," I agree in a heartbeat. "How's Saturday?"

"Saturday works."

We spend the rest of lunch talking about our favorite graphic novels. Before we leave, we exchange phone numbers so he can text me his address.

"I'll see you Saturday then," I say as we step out onto the sidewalk.

"In the meantime, keep your eyes on the road and don't step in front of any buses," he advises with a smirk.

CHAPTER 4

Easton

I have no idea what I was thinking inviting River here, except that once we got past the *massively* awkward part, he was actually pretty cool to talk to. I shouldn't have even agreed to have lunch with him. It's too weird, too complicated, but it was impossible to say no to the chance to get to know him.

No matter what Fox said, I needed to see for myself that this man was worthy of having a piece of Paul. And after meeting him, I can't regret the decision I made. I wouldn't have traded Paul for anyone or anything in the world, but the fact of the matter is, Paul was dead one way or the other—at least he was able to save River's life. Paul would've liked knowing that. He would probably say it gave his death more meaning. I comfort myself with these things even as my own heart aches with missing my husband.

I spend most of the morning fidgeting and tidying the house in between trying to get my next novel started. I plotted it out before I finished the last one, but every time I sit down to try to work on the first panel, I think of something else I can clean or straighten or rearrange and get up to do that instead.

At two o'clock on the dot, there's a knock at the front door that starts my heart pounding wildly against my ribcage. I wipe my sweat damp palms on my jeans and take a deep breath before answering it.

"Hi," I greet River with a smile, determined not to leave him with the impression that I'm a perpetually weepy, morose person. Although, how long does something have to be a habit before it becomes who you are?

He looks a bit awestruck as he stares at me from the front porch with a computer bag over one shoulder and a huge smile on his lips. "I can't believe I'm at Easton Harrison's house. The guys on the EH forum would lose their shit if they heard about this."

"I'm sorry, the what?" I ask, stepping aside to let him in.

A blush stains his cheeks. "It's nothing, just this fan forum where we talk about your books."

"Wow, you're like a proper fanboy," I say with a laugh.

"Just a little," he confesses, pinching his thumb and forefinger half an inch apart to illustrate his point. Taking off his shoes and leaving them on the mat just inside the door, he sets his computer bag gently on the floor beside them and steps farther into the house.

We stand looking at each other for a few awkward seconds, neither of us sure what to say or do next. I can feel a thread of connection to him, if only in my imagination, but we're still strangers. It's a dichotomy I don't know how to navigate, and I have to wonder why River agreed to come here. He doesn't know about the connection we share, so is it just about being a fan of my work?

"Do you want something to drink?" I offer.

"I'm good, thanks." He shifts from one foot to the other, lifting one hand to the back of his neck and rubbing it absently.

"I'm going to grab my old work to show you," I say, waving him into the house.

River follows me down the hallway to the spare bedroom where my box of original, unpublished work lives—the same bedroom where all Paul's things are stored. We step inside, and I swear I can feel River's eyes as he takes in the clutter of boxes.

"Sorry, this room is kind of a mess," I apologize.

"Dude, you should see my place," he laughs off the apology. "These your husband's things?" he guesses as I move a couple of boxes to get to the one I need.

"Yes. I know I should get rid of them, but..."

"You don't have to grieve on anyone else's schedule," he says firmly. "Get rid of them when it feels right or keep them forever; it's not anyone's call but yours."

"I'm not sure my therapist would agree but thank you."

River frowns. "Your therapist is pushing you to toss everything?"

"Well, no, not at first," I admit. "But five years is a long time to stay married to a dead man." I finally find the box I need and try to pick it up, but it's heavier than I remember it being. I grunt and wobble with it in my arms, River swooping in quickly to relieve me of it.

"Careful," he says, taking the box into his own arms, his muscles straining against the sleeves of his t-shirt. He's not overly built, but he certainly has a nice physique. Now that he's wearing a t-shirt instead of a suit, I can see that his arms are covered in tattoos, beautiful colors snaking around his arms in an inviting way. My stomach flutters for an entirely different reason than nerves for the first time in five years, and I feel instantly guilty.

"I know he's gone," I say, partially to distract myself from River's biceps. "I just keep waiting for it to get easier. Isn't time supposed to heal this kind of thing?"

"I don't think time heals a loss like this," he says. "I think over time you just learn how to live with the pain of it."

I lead River back into the living room so he doesn't have to stand around holding such a heavy box, not that he seems to be having much trouble with it.

"Have you lost someone close?" I ask. He certainly seems familiar with the pain of it.

"My dad died when I was sixteen. I still miss him a lot."

"I'm sorry," I offer, and River waves it off.

I direct him to set the box down next to the couch, and we both sit down. It's been years since I've opened this box up to look at my old work, so it's a little dusty as I pull the flaps open. We both cough, and I laugh apologetically.

"Holy shit," River says, his eyes landing on the contents of the box. "Can I?" he checks, and I nod for him to go ahead. He reaches in and gingerly picks up the top book. It's bound in nothing fancier than a three-ring binder with the title hastily scrawled on the front. He flips it open, and his eyes get even wider.

I crane my neck to see which one this is, smiling when I remember the short story featuring a psychic paranormal cop. It was silly and fairly cliché, and the drawings slightly rougher as I was finding my style, but I had fun writing it. Paul claimed he loved it, reading each new page before bed every night until it was finished.

"This is awesome," he says as he flips through it carefully, only gingerly gripping the edge of each sheet of paper and gently turning them. "I mean, I can tell it's early work because your drawing style isn't the same as it is now, but it's still really good."

"Thank you." I smile and sit back, enjoying

his excitement over the chance to read my unpublished, early work. "I always saw it as a pipe dream to have them published, but Paul pushed me to pursue it anyway."

"What did you do before you were published? Did you have another job you left?"

"I was an art teacher. I still volunteer to teach some classes at the community center downtown."

"That's so cool. When I was trying to decide on a major, I wanted to stick with graphic art, but my parents were so worried I'd become a starving artist, I ended up compromising and getting my degree in marketing with a minor in graphic design. Don't get me wrong, it's a great combination of degrees to have. The graphic art aspect makes me a lot better at marketing, but sometimes I wish I could spend more time creating art for the sake of art, you know?"

"I get it."

He sets down the psychic detective and picks up a different one, this time about a young boy dealing with his emerging werewolf side. I wrote it with strong undertones of the struggle to accept yourself as a teenager and coming out of the closet. Again, it's a bit cliché and maybe a tad heavy handed, but it was another fun one to write.

He takes his time looking through each book, asking questions and gushing over each one. I look at the clock and realize the afternoon has really gotten away from us.

"Are you hungry? I promised to feed you and then got caught up letting you shower me with praise instead," I joke.

"Yeah, I could eat." He looks up from the final book, closing it and setting it carefully back into the box with the others.

"Great, I'll order something. What do you like? Anything you don't eat?"

"I'm kind of a pain in the ass with my diet," he says apologetically. "I don't eat red meat and nothing high in trans-fat or really greasy."

"That's okay. Actually, I have fish I bought fresh yesterday that I was planning to cook tomorrow, but if you want, I'd be happy to grill it up tonight instead."

"I don't want to put you out."

"It's no trouble. Honestly, I kind of miss cooking for someone other than myself," I admit.

"Okay, if you're sure, then that sounds great."

River

Easton sets to work lighting the grill outside on the back patio and then preparing the fish along with a side of asparagus. I'm still trying to wrap my head around how surreal this day has been. Having the chance to see his early work lit a spark of hope inside me that maybe someday I'll finish a graphic novel worth publishing.

"So, tell me more about your job in marketing," he prompts after putting the food on the grill.

"I'm not sure there's much to tell. Companies hire us to create ads or marketing plans for them, and then we do it. It's a challenge sometimes but it's fun."

"Have you worked on a big, famous ad campaign I would know?" He pulls a bottle of wine out of the refrigerator and grabs two glasses.

"Oh sorry, I don't drink," I tell him quickly. "And I'm not sure I would call any of the campaigns I've done *famous*. With my graphic design background, I'm usually put in charge of new logos and things."

"That sounds fun," he says. "The drinking and the diet, is that all because of the heart transplant?" he asks casually, but there's a hint of a deeper curiosity in his eyes.

"Yeah, it was a long shot to get this heart; I'm not about to risk doing anything to damage it because I don't see getting another one. Plus, it's probably silly, but I feel like I need to respect the donor, and the best way I know how to do that is to treat it like gold."

"I'm sure that means a lot to the donor's family," Easton says, his voice a little choked up. He takes a sip of wine, and then his steel-gray eyes meet mine, holding my gaze hostage. "Do you know anything about them?"

"About who?"

"The family of the donor," he clarifies.

"No. The hospital gave me the opportunity

to write a thank you letter that they delivered, but because of HIPPA and everything I don't even know a name or anything about the donor."

"Oh." He takes another sip of his wine, his throat bobbing as he swallows, his grip on the stem tight, but I swear a hint of relief flickers in his eyes. "The fish is going to take a little while to cook, do you want to show me the graphic novel you've been working on?"

"Yeah," I agree, hurrying over to grab my computer bag with my laptop and tablet inside. My hands tremble slightly as I place it on the counter and unzip it. I've never shown this to *anyone* before. Brandon knows about my hobby, but I've refused to show him, no matter how much he's begged and teased about it.

I take out my tablet and pull up the file, my heart going wild as I pass it across the island to Easton. I hold my breath as he picks it up and starts to look through it. Different expressions flicker over his face as his eyes move over the screen from panel to panel.

I'm sure any artist can attest there's nothing more nerve wracking than letting someone see your work for the first time. I feel like I'm standing completely naked in front of this man I only just met. Not that I've ever stood naked in front of a man before to know what that feels like...not that I haven't thought about it a time or two...that's *so* not the point right now. I take a deep breath and try to calm my awkward and racing thoughts.

I focus instead on Easton's expression as he continues to study the screen in front of him, a small smile forming on his mouth. That has to be a good thing, right?

"Okay, you're killing me over here," I admit. "What do you think?"

He sets my tablet down and looks up at me, his gray eyes ensnaring mine in his penetrating gaze.

"Do you want my honest opinion?"

"Only if it won't make me cry," I joke.

"I think you have a ton of promise. This is fantastic, and I honestly think with a little more practice and a bit of mentoring you could absolutely finish a marketable graphic novel that a publisher would be dying to get their hands on."

"Seriously?" I ask breathlessly, happiness fizzing through me.

"I don't say things I don't mean, River."

"Wow, that's...wow." I know I sound like an idiot but try having one of your heroes tell you they think you have promise, and see if you can form a response that makes you sound like a genius.

CHAPTER 5

River

I find myself smiling through the rest of the weekend, replaying the night with Easton on a loop. After he blew my mind by telling me my work had promise, we spent the rest of the evening discussing our favorite artists as well as which graphic novels we've enjoyed the most. Before I knew it, it was nearly midnight, and I'd dragged myself home reluctantly.

My good mood has lasted all the way through Monday morning as I send off my latest logo and branding mock-up to my boss for approval and then look up to see Brandon standing in my office door with two coffee cups in his hands.

"Hey," I greet him with a nod.

"Hey," he says, stepping in and setting one of the cups on my desk. "Decaf."

"Thank you." I reach for it and take a sip. "How was your weekend?"

"Great. I had a third date with Jeanine that lasted all the way through Sunday afternoon," he says, waggling his eyebrows suggestively.

"Poor girl," I tease.

"Speaking of which, have you taken a vow of celibacy or what?" he jokes back, arching an eyebrow at me.

I groan and tilt my head back, running my hands over my face and then through my hair.

"I don't know, man. I'm just...tired."

"Tired?" he repeats skeptically, a hint of concern creeping into his eyes like he's afraid I'm about to keel over.

"Yeah, tired of forcing a connection where there isn't one, tired of telling myself I feel something I don't. I want to feel something real for someone."

"Riv, I mean this in the nicest possible way, but you sound like a total pussy right now."

"Dude," I scold, "having feelings does not make me a pussy. You're buying into the bullshit stereotypes that men aren't supposed to have feelings."

"I love you, but you're a pain in the ass," Brandon says with a laugh. "Do you think..."

"What? Just say it, man; I'm sure I won't think you're more of a dick than I already do."

"Well, way back in college you told me you were into guys too, but have you ever dated any guys?"

My heart beats a little faster. "No." The truth is, being bi is something I figured out as a teen, but it's always been *in theory*. I can appreciate a hot dude. Sometimes I'll be in the mood to jerk it to gay porn instead of straight, but the thought of actually dating or fooling around with a guy is intimidating as hell. I never even meant to tell Brandon that I'm bi; I haven't told anyone else. But during our senior year of college, he borrowed my laptop and saw a tab I accidentally left open for a gay porn site.

He came to me the next day and told me he didn't care if I was gay. I freaked a little that I'd been found out when I wasn't anywhere near ready to discuss it. But he was understanding when I told him I wasn't gay, I was bi, and that I'd rather we didn't talk any more about it. He hasn't brought it up again in the last nine years...until now.

"Maybe you should try that out," he suggests with a shrug.

"Maybe," I agree noncommittally, taking a sip of my drink to combat my suddenly dry mouth, images of Easton's sweet half-smile flickering through my mind.

"I just want to see you happy. Personally, I don't see why you're so hung up on the idea of settling down, but if that's your joy, then more power to you." And *that's* why Brandon is my best friend.

Easton

I stare out the back window of my kitchen, Paul's favorite mug in my hand, contemplating the patch of dirt where my garden used to be. I swear I can still see Paul out there, sweaty and shirtless as he diligently created the garden spot, turning up the hard dirt with a shovel and adding the nutrient rich soil he'd gone out and bought for me. If I knew Paul, he'd likely asked every employee at the garden shop which brand was best before choosing one.

I spent hours out in that garden, tending to the flowers I planted and pulling weeds while Paul watched me from the deck with a smile on his face.

Of course, I haven't touched it since the day Paul died. It's overgrown and full of weeds, it's the perfect allegory for my life without Paul—something that used to be beautiful is now just sad.

My phone chimes in my pocket, and I pull it out to see a text from River.

River: I'm not sure if we're like friends or our recent hang out was a one-time thing, but every Sunday I like to check out all the art vendors along the Riverwalk, and I thought you might want to join me?

I stare at the words on the screen for several seconds. I should turn him down. Yes, we had fun hanging out the other night, but I should leave it at that. I know I should leave it at that. But my fingers seem to have a mind of their own as I type my response.

Easton: I haven't been in years, I'd love to

I hold my breath as soon as I hit send, guilt and excitement warring as I watch the little dots bounce as River types back again.

River: Great! I'll see you Sunday then
Easton: See you then

I catch myself smiling as I slip my phone back into my pocket. Maybe Fox was right, I've spent long enough locked away in my house mourning Paul. I used to love seeing all the artists on the Riverwalk, waking up early on purpose on Sundays to get there early. It's time to start living again, if only in this small way.

I glance back out the window one more time at my sad excuse for a garden and for the first time in five years, I see the possibilities there. I could pull the weeds, clear out the dead flowers, and replace them with life. Unlike Paul, my garden could live again...*I* could live again.

I dump my cooling tea into the sink and carefully hand wash the mug before setting it in the drying rack, and then I return to my office to get back to work.

When my phone rings a few hours later, my heart gives a funny jolt, thinking it might be River. Which is obviously the silliest thing ever. I see Fox's name on the screen and guilt swamps over me. He didn't even want to find River for me, and he didn't want to tell me any more than absolutely necessary about him, I can't imagine he'd be thrilled to know I'm hanging out with him now.

I almost don't answer, sure the guilt will end up getting the better of me, and I'll spill everything to him. But if I don't answer, he'll likely get worried and drive over here anyway. Better to get it over with.

"Hey, Fox," I say, cringing at my overly cheerful tone. He's clearly as put off by it as I am because he doesn't say anything back for several long seconds.

"Hey, East," he finally responds, somewhat warily. "How's it going?"

"It's going. What's up?"

"Just checking in on you."

His words draw me up short. How had I not realized until this moment what a chore I'd become to the people around me? And by people around me, I mean Fox, because I've long since pushed everyone else away.

"I'm fine. You don't have to worry about me."

He makes a disbelieving sound in the back of his throat. "Have you been holding up your end of the bargain?" he asks. "Getting out of the house? Spending time with the living."

"Yes," I answer honestly, cringing to myself at the thought of what he would say if he knew *who* I was spending time with. I have no doubt Fox would find a way to say it's wrong, that it's my way of not letting go of Paul. And maybe at first that was part of it, but spending time with him over the weekend, talking about graphic design and sharing dinner, it didn't feel like I was thinking of him as a connection to Paul, he just felt like River.

"Good, I'm glad to hear that, East. It's what Paul would've wanted."

"I know."

CHAPTER 6

River

The sun heats my skin as I stand on the sidewalk just shy of the art fair, my hands in my pockets, and a smile on my lips, people watching while I wait for Easton. There's a lightness in my chest that's become unfamiliar lately. I don't know if it's the chance to spend more time with Easton or the fact that I spent all my free time in the past week working on my art, inspired after my chat with Easton and all his encouragement. I've started imagining a life where my art could be the focus instead of sitting in an office making logos for other people.

I catch sight of Easton coming down the sidewalk, his messy curls bouncing with each stride, the sun kissing his face and making his skin glow a beautiful golden hue. The corners of his lips are upturned ever so slightly. Probably not something I would even notice if not for the fact that both times I've seen him so far, his rare smiles have seemed forced. This is relaxed, it's genuine, and it's one of the most breathtaking things I've ever seen. My heart beats faster the closer Easton comes, almost as if it's trying to leap out of my chest to greet him.

"Hi," he says when he reaches me, his voice all shy sweetness, a light blush pinking his cheeks.

"Hi."

We stare at each other for several seconds, and I wonder if it's possible he can hear how loudly my heart is pounding. The strangest urge to grab his hand and put it against my chest nearly overwhelms me, and I have to wonder if I'm completely losing my mind. Am I attracted to Easton? Is that all this is? Is this a fucked-up kind of hero worship because I love his work and he saved my life? Does it matter what it really is, or should I ride it and see where it goes?

"I always loved the weekly art fair. I'm a little mad at myself that it's been so long since I've come," he says, breaking the confusing tension.

I glance over my shoulder at the tables and tents of art vendors lining the Riverwalk.

"I love this place. I almost never buy anything, but it's like my happy place. No matter how long or stressful my week is, no matter what kind of moody funk I get myself into, coming here is like a vacation." I study Easton's face, trying to gauge just how weird that made me sound, but he smiles.

"I like that, it's nice."

I nod, shifting on my feet. "Shall we?" I ask nodding toward the fair.

"Yeah."

We walk close together, side by side. Our

arms or hands brush every so often, each time sending a little sizzle of awareness through me. As we make our way from booth to booth, taking in art from dozens of artists, I find myself engrossed with the emotions that pass over Easton's face with each one. He doesn't just *look* at any single painting or piece of art, he feels it. I notice paintings of flowers are his favorite, his face lighting up and a little dimple appearing in his left cheek when he looks at these. Sometimes the happiness is short lived, his lips turning down after a few seconds and a glassiness clouding his eyes. I wonder if they remind him of Paul.

I swear I could watch him all afternoon long, and I decide I don't want to try to figure out what to make of that—I just want to experience it. So what if I'm developing a tiny crush on Easton? If anything, he might be the perfect first man for me to swoon over. He's clearly still deeply in love with his late husband, so the intimidation factor is non-existent. Nothing will come of this. I'm free to just *feel* it.

At the next stall, Easton stops in front of a small oil painting of a field of wildflowers, the colors so vibrant they seem to jump off the canvas. He stares, mesmerized for several minutes, and I study him the same way he does the painting. I wonder if I look at him long enough if I'll be able to peel back the layer of loss and sadness that clings to him like a second skin and find out who the man beneath truly is.

He reaches out as if he's going to touch the painting, stopping short with his fingertips a hair from it. He lets out a sigh, his shoulders slumping before he pulls his hand back and looks over at me with a sad smile.

"I miss my colors," he admits, and my heart gives another stupid little flutter. I hardly know this man; why in the world should it matter to me that he's sharing a secret part of himself? I don't have a good answer, but it makes me feel special, nevertheless.

"Where'd they go?" I ask gently.

"They're all wrapped around Paul, and I can't untangle them. Red isn't red anymore. It's the way I loved him and his favorite color. And the hard hat that didn't protect him. Green isn't green. It's how jealous I would get when other men would hit on him, the color he wanted to paint our bedroom, and the garden he helped me plant. Blue isn't blue. It's the loneliness of missing him, his eyes, and the color of his lips after they took him off life support." He chokes out a sob, putting a hand over his mouth as his shoulders start to shake with his muffled cries. A few people turn to look, the artist of the painting looking thoroughly alarmed by the weeping man in his booth.

I put my arms around Easton and make a soothing noise in my throat, rubbing my hand up and down his back while I hold him tightly with the other arm, doing my best to calm him. He buries his face against my shoulder, soaking the fabric of my shirt with his tears.

"I'm sorry," he sniffles, trying to push out of my arms. I tighten my grip around him for a second, not wanting to let him go for some reason, and then reluctantly release him.

He steps back and wipes the backs of his hands across his tear stained cheeks, sniffling again. The skin on his face and throat is splotchy red, tears still clinging to his long, dark eyelashes, his eyes red rimmed. As ill-advised as it seems, I reach out and run my thumb over his cheek to gather a few last stray tears.

"You must think I'm a complete fucking basket case," he says with disgust.

"I think you're someone who suffered a huge loss and is still trying to find a way to cope with it."

"At some point I need to just get the fuck over it. Paul is gone, and he's never coming back," he says sternly as if scolding himself.

"Don't be so hard on yourself."

He sniffles once more and then straightens his shoulders.

"I'm hungry. Do you want to go somewhere for breakfast?" he asks, the change of subject so unexpected it nearly gives me whiplash.

"Yeah, let's go for breakfast," I agree. As we walk away from the booth, I glance back at the painting that sent him into tears. I wish there was a way I could give him his colors back, that I could make his world beautiful again for him.

Easton

By the time we reach the little cafe a few blocks over, the tears have dried from my face, and the sadness has passed. Now I'm just feeling embarrassed. Embarrassed I cried all over his shirt, embarrassed I broke down so completely in front of him, and embarrassed of what River must think of me.

I never used to be this weepy person. Some days I miss laid back, vibrant, artist Easton as much as I miss Paul. Sometimes, when I can't sleep, I lay awake in the dark of my bedroom all alone and try to remember that person, to remember what it felt like to embrace life so fully, to laugh and love and fucking live.

My eyes start to burn again, and I rapidly blink the forming tears away. *I'm not crying anymore today*, I resolve.

"I've never been in here," River says as we step inside the cozy cafe Paul and I used to frequent on lazy weekends.

"The blueberry muffins are *amazing*. I'd basically sell my first-born child for one."

River snorts a laugh. "Normally muffins aren't in my diet, but with an endorsement like that, how can I resist?"

"Why don't you grab a table, I'll order," I suggest. "Do you drink coffee?"

"No. Orange juice sounds good. Thanks."

River claims a table near the window, and I get our food and drinks.

"Sorry again for the crying thing," I say as I slide his muffin and orange juice across the table to him.

He waves me off. "Seriously, don't worry about it."

"I have this garden," I say. I'm not sure why, but I feel like I want to open up to him, I want River to know me. "Well, *had* this garden. I swear I could lose entire days outside pulling weeds, planting flowers, just being surrounded by the butterflies and blooms."

"You don't garden anymore?"

I shake my head. "It's all ugly and overgrown now. I'd need to pull everything out and start from scratch; it's a huge project."

"Sometimes a complete overhaul is exactly what you need," River says wisely.

"Maybe you're right." The thought of weeding Paul's ghost from my life and planting an entirely new garden in its place is both terrifying and thrilling. I'm not sure I've ever wanted and dreaded the idea of anything more in my life. Maybe it's time.

"Hey, East." Fox's voice startles me into nearly spilling my tea as I lift it to my lips. My eyes go wide when I spot him over River's shoulder, coming closer with a half-smile tilting his lips, his eyes darting between the back of River's head and my face.

"Hey, Fox," I reply, taking a sip of tea to moisten my dry throat. My heart pounds out a violent tattoo against my ribcage. When he sees River's face, he's going to know exactly who he is.

I hold my breath as River turns to see him. Fox's smile falters, his eyes flicking to mine and then back to River several times before he forces another smile, barely more than a grimace and holds his hand out.

"Sorry to interrupt, I'm Fox."

"River," he says back, shaking Fox's hand and then squinting his eyes at him. "Have we met before? You look really familiar."

Oh shit. I chew my lip and beg Fox with my eyes not to tell River we're connected.

"I think I just have one of those faces," Fox offers easily, and River seems to take that as enough of an explanation.

"Mind if I talk to you for just a second, East?"

"Sure." I grit my teeth and push back from the table, following Fox outside.

As soon as we're on the sidewalk, he spins on me. "What the actual fuck?"

"What?" I reply as innocently as possible.

"Cut the shit," he grinds out between his clenched teeth. "You can't fucking do this. What even is this? Does he know about Paul? I mean seriously, East, what the fuck?"

"It wasn't intentional," I defend. "I was on my way back from dropping off my finished book with my agent when I saw him. I wasn't going to talk to him or anything, but then he nearly got flattened by a bus. If I hadn't stepped in, he'd be dead right now."

"Does he know about Paul?" Fox asks again.

"He knows I had a husband who died, that's it. And I'm not planning to tell him anything else."

"So what, you're *dating* him now? You have to see how messed up that is."

"I'm not dating him. We're...*friends*. At least I think we're friends."

"Jesus Christ," he mutters, pinching the bridge of his nose. "I get that you've had a hard time dealing with Paul's death, we all have. I've done everything in my power to take care of you the way he would've wanted me to. But this is too far, East. I can't stand by and let you do this."

"It's not how you're thinking," I defend. "You don't get it."

"You need—"

"I need to get back to my tea before it gets cold," I cut him off. "I appreciate your opinion, but I have to do this."

"Do *what*?" Fox asks again. "I don't even get what this is."

"I don't know either," I admit. "I'll talk to you later." I turn and go back into the cafe.

River is picking apart the muffin and popping pieces into his mouth and scrolling through his phone when I get back to the table.

"Everything cool?" he asks when I pull my chair out and plop down, reaching for my tea and taking a sip.

"Yeah, sorry about that."

"Not gonna lie, that was kind of weird. Are you dating that guy? Was he jealous or something?"

"Fox? God no," I shake my head furiously and chuckle at the thought. "He was Paul's best friend."

"So, he *was* jealous, just for his friend instead of himself."

"I guess so," I agree, deciding that's probably the easiest explanation.

"I don't want to cause problems between you guys."

"He'll get over it," I assure him.

"Does that mean you want to keep hanging out?" His voice is hopeful and slightly vulnerable. If I hadn't already decided that I wanted to keep spending time with River, this would've convinced me.

"I like hanging out with you."

"Me too."

"I guess that makes us friends then," I add, feeling a little like a child on the playground, desperate to know he wants to be my friend.

"We're friends," River agrees. "I have a feeling we're going to become good friends."

"Me too."

CHAPTER 7

River

I step off the elevator onto my floor at work on Monday morning with a little extra bounce in my step. After having breakfast at the cafe on Sunday, we went back to Easton's house again and spent a majority of the day watching obscure Japanese anime with terrible dubbing. He cooked dinner again, a roast chicken and vegetables to stick to my strict diet, and we talked for quite a while. When it was time to finally leave, it felt like such a shame to go. I wanted to find more reasons to linger, more ways to get him to open up, more ways to make his lips twitch in an almost smile.

Even thinking of him has my heart doing backflips.

I get to my office and boot up my computer. I have a random lock screen that changes each time I restart the computer, and this morning it's a field of wildflowers, and I think of Easton instantly, a rush of warm affection going through me.

Last night after I finally got home, instead of going straight to bed, I stayed up drawing out a few panels of a new graphic novel. Easton's words had echoed in my head. *I miss my colors.* I couldn't stop thinking about it, about how it must feel to suffer a loss so big that everything else becomes flat and lifeless. That thought fueled a creative frenzy as I'd hastily roughed out a plot and then started to draw.

I'd been up far too late, hunched over a Tablet until my eyes burned and my hand started to cramp, but I went to bed feeling excited.

I spend the next few hours getting my work done, thoughts of Easton constantly attempting to invade my brain, my hand twitching for my phone on more than one occasion, wanting to text him and tell him about my new graphic novel.

A tap at my door draws my attention, and I glance at the clock and realize it's lunch time already.

"Ready to grab something to eat?" Brandon asks, leaning against my door frame.

"Yeah, I completely lost track of time. Let me save what I'm working on, and we can go."

It's a warm day again, the sun beating down on us as we walk down the street to our favorite little deli.

"I tried to call you yesterday to see if you wanted to hit the gym together."

"Oh, sorry, I was out all day."

"Really?" he says, sounding far too intrigued. "Where were you?"

"Just hanging out with a friend," I say with a shrug.

"No offense, man, but who do you hang out with aside from me?"

"People," I lie, feeling my cheeks heat up.

"You had a date," he accuses entirely too gleefully.

"It wasn't a date," I grumble.

"But you wanted it to be," he says, not backing down. "Who was she?"

"It was a he actually," I mumble.

"*Interesting*," he says, stroking his chin in an exaggerated fashion. "Tell me about him."

"I don't know; there's not much to say. We met like two weeks ago, and we've hung out a couple of times. It's no big deal."

"If you don't want to tell me about it that's fine, but I'm here if you *do* want to," he assures me, clapping me on the shoulder as we step into the deli.

"You really wouldn't mind that? If I *was* dating a guy, you'd really want to hear about it?"

"I mean, I don't need all the details, but if it was someone who made you happy, I'd definitely want to know about them, whatever gender they are."

"Thanks, man."

"That's what friends are for."

The subject moves off my sex life for the rest of lunch, and by the time I get back to my desk, I can't resist the urge to text Easton any longer.

River: Hey, what are you doing tonight?

Easton: Nothing.

River: There's this hibachi grill I've been dying to try, want to join me?

I cringe as soon as I hit send, realizing immediately how date-ish that invite sounded. The little bouncing dots pop up to let me know he's typing, then they stop, and then start again. This repeats several times until I'm torn between texting back *never mind* or calling him and asking him to answer the damn question and put me out of my misery already.

Easton

I read the text several times over, typing and erasing half a dozen responses. River and I said we were friends, and I have no reason to think this invitation is anything but that. Except…a hibachi feels like a date. I've never had a friend invite me to a hibachi, unless it was for my birthday.

I'm sure River isn't looking at this as a date. I don't even know if he's into guys. For all I know, he's straight as an arrow and really passionate about watching his food be cooked in front of him.

I type *sure* and then delete it.

But what if he is *trying to ask me on a date?* My chest constricts at the thought, my stomach going all funny and squirmy. I can't date. And even if I *could*, dating River would be way too fucked up. Just look at how Fox reacted yesterday when he thought I was on a date with River. I can only imagine how River would feel finding out about the connection we share. It's weird, it's way too weird.

Not tonight, I type and then delete it.

Maybe I'm overthinking this. Fox was right about one thing: I've spent entirely too long hiding out in my house, acting like I died when Paul did. Five years is more than enough time to hold a living memorial to the man I loved more than anything. It's time I start living again, and dinner with a friend is harmless.

Easton: Sounds fun! What time?

River: 7? I'll text you the address, and you can meet me there?

I blow out a breath. Not a date then. If it was a date, he'd pick me up, right? That's still proper these days, isn't it? Not that I'd know. I've been out of the dating world for nearly fifteen years. I was only twenty-one when Paul and I met. We fell in love fast and never looked back. I never believed in soulmates, but Paul made me question that. He made me feel like we were two halves of one whole, utterly entwined with each other.

Of course River wasn't asking me on a date. I shake my head and laugh at myself. Even if River *was* into men, why in the world would he be interested in me. So far all I've done is cry all over him and act like a general bummer.

I pass the afternoon getting some work

done, occasionally getting up to stretch my legs and wandering to the back window to look out at my sad, overgrown patch of garden. River was right; sometimes the best thing you can do is rip everything out by its roots and start from scratch. I just don't know if I'm ready to do that yet.

When seven o'clock gets near, I change into clean clothes and head downtown to meet River.

He's waiting outside the restaurant when I get there, wearing a blue suit similar to the one he was wearing the first day we met. It's perfectly tailored, accentuating his broad shoulders and fitting him like a dream. My heart beats a little faster, my mouth going dry, and, to my surprise, heat starts to stir in the pit of my stomach, spreading between my legs.

It's not like my dick shriveled up and fell off five years ago, but there hasn't been a specific person who's stirred anything in me in all this time. It's been more like a matter of maintenance. I throw on some porn and jerk off when I'm in the mood, but other than that, it's the last thing on my mind. I can't actually even remember how long it's been since I've even done that. Two weeks? Three? Longer than that?

River looks up and our eyes meet, butterflies going wild in my stomach. I swallow hard and smile at him. I can't be attracted to River. I *can't*.

"Hey," he says. "Glad you came, I thought it would be way too pathetic to come here alone."

"Thanks for inviting me."

River holds open the door for me and ushers me inside. The smell of cooked meat and the sizzle of the grills fills the air as we enter, and a little spark of excitement goes through me. I haven't been out to do anything fun like this in so long. A little part of the old Easton feels like he's waking up inside me after a too long sleep. Is it possible that part of me isn't dead? That it was only hibernating?

We're seated at a table with a handful of other people, and we enjoy the show the chef puts on, flipping things into the air with the tip of his knife, making a smoke volcano with a stack of onions.

River leans close, and his breath tickles my ear, sending a little shiver over my skin as goosebumps erupt.

"You have a really nice smile."

I turn my head, and my breath catches when I realize just how close he really is, our noses only a few inches apart. I can hear my blood whooshing in my ears making all the other sounds of the restaurant fade to a muffled murmur. Time seems to stand still for several confusing, heart pounding seconds. And then River clears his throat and jerks back.

Just like that, the room seems to come back into focus, sound rushing loudly around me as I blink rapidly and try to get my bearings.

Needing something to do other than stare at River or fall apart, I turn back to my food and pick up my fork with a trembling hand. I take slow, steady breaths, holding each one in my lungs for several seconds before exhaling and telling myself over and over that I am *not* going to freak out.

River chats happily beside me as if nothing happened, going on about something I don't have the current mental capacity to decipher. Maybe Fox was right, spending time with River can't possibly lead anywhere good.

I'm not sure I manage to string two more words together for the rest of the meal, nodding absently and numbly shoveling food into my mouth, all the while a storm rages inside me, threatening to spill over.

River walks me back to the car, and outside the noise of the restaurant, the silence stretching between us becomes even more pronounced. I listen to the slap and scrape of each footstep we take into the parking lot, counting my breaths, and focusing on holding it together.

"Thanks for coming to dinner with me," River says with a hint of uncertainty when we reach my car.

"Thanks for inviting me," I manage to reply through a dry throat.

"I'll talk to you later?"

"Mmhmm," I hum, nodding and avoiding meeting his eyes for fear they'll somehow ensnare me again, drawing me in and making me feel things that are supposed to belong to Paul. My throat constricts at the thought and I dip my head, reaching for the door handle and slipping into my car without looking back at him. I'm not sure if he walks away or watches me drive off, but I feel like I can sense the weight of his gaze on me all the way home.

As soon as I'm home, I collapse into bed, clutching a pillow to my chest and crying deep, body wracking sobs that turn my throat raw and make it impossible to breathe. I would give any- thing for Paul to put his arms around me and tell me everything is going to be okay. I press my face into the pillow that was once his and imagine I can still smell him there. My heart aches for him like a missing limb.

How could I entertain even the *thought* of someone else? Is it because River has a part of Paul, or is there something about River himself turning my head around?

I can't see him again, I resolve when I man- age to calm down enough to stop crying. But even with that promise to myself, I can't stop feeling like I betrayed Paul, like I almost cheated on him.

Without thinking, I reach for my phone and call Fox.

"Hello?" he answers, and I sniffle into the phone. "East, are you okay? What's wrong?"

"You were right," I admit miserably.

"I usually am. But what was I right about this time?"

"I almost kissed him tonight. I wanted things I had no right wanting. Paul would hate me right now. He'd feel so betrayed. I'm the worst person alive." Tears start to fall again, and I choke on a fresh sob.

"Hey, whoa, East, listen to me," Fox says in that calm voice he's perfected in the past five years. "River aside, you've kept yourself in mourning for Paul for longer than he ever would have expected or wanted. You're only thirty-five, do you honestly think he would've wanted you to stay alone the rest of your life?"

I take that as a rhetorical question because we both know Paul was a hopeless romantic. He would've hated the idea of *anyone* being alone, least of all me.

"How could there ever be anyone else for me? Paul was perfect."

"I know," he soothes. "But at least leave your heart open for it, because you never know, lightning might strike twice."

"Fine," I agree reluctantly. "But I'm not going to hang out with River again; you were right about that."

"If that's what you think is best."

"It is. I'm going to go to sleep now I think."

"Okay," he says. "Are you going to be all right or do you want me to come over?"

I'm ashamed to admit how many nights Fox has held me while I've cried myself to sleep.

"I'll be fine. Thanks for listening."

"Any time."

We hang up, and I burrow under my blankets, pulling Paul's pillow close to my face again and closing my eyes, exhaustion from my crying fit overtaking me.

CHAPTER 8

River

Our bodies slide against each other—all hard planes and coarse hair, open mouths bumping against each other in the approximation of a kiss as desperate moans fall from his lips into mine. The taste of his tongue lingers on mine, and pleasure rolls up my spine as the hot, silky steel of his erection humps against mine.

"River." My name like a prayer, his body bowing up to meet mine.

"Easton," I moan, the taste of his name on my tongue sending a rush of pleasure through me. "Easton," I gasp again, fucking against him faster, grunting as my balls ache and tighten. "Easton," I groan as my muscles tense, and I spill my release all over his already heated skin, cum and sweat mixing together and sticking us together.

I wake with a gasp, my fist wrapped around my erection, cum pulsing out and spilling over my fingers.

"Fuck," I pant, clenching my eyes closed tightly, my chest rising and falling rapidly with harsh breaths, my stomach muscles tense, and my heart fluttering. I roll over and reach blindly for my dirty shirt, lying on the floor beside the bed and use it to clean myself up. Then I sit with my face in my hands, attempting to get my thoughts together and my heart to stop beating so hard.

I'm thirty years old; I should've left wet dreams behind in my teens. My body is still buzzing as my mind continues to supply snapshots of the dream, keeping my erection from fully going down.

There was a moment at the restaurant last night when I thought for a second Easton might kiss me. He'd been close enough that I'd been able to feel his breath ghosting over my lips. But I panicked. I wanted it so badly it terrified me. Never in my life have I looked at another person and felt like if I didn't feel their lips on mine, I might actually die from wanting.

Easton grew quiet after that while I dealt with my discomfort with an unending stream of chatter that lasted the rest of the meal, leaving me to wonder if he was upset that I freaked out or upset about the moment between us.

Throwing back my blanket, I swing my feet over the side of the bed and get up. The sky is gray through the windows, the barest hints of morning light starting to peek over the horizon as I shuffle to the kitchen to pour myself a glass of water.

After I guzzle down a glass of water, the last thing I want to do is go back to bed. My body is still wired, thoughts of Easton filling my mind. So, instead, I grab my Tablet and stylus and sit down at my kitchen table.

It's impossible not to think of Easton while I work. After all, the story was inspired by him.

Eventually, morning sun is shining through the windows, and I have to pull myself away from my sketches to get ready for my actual job. But Easton never leaves my mind.

Easton

I spend the week buried in working on my next book and thinking about little else. On Monday I pick up my phone and consider calling River over and over, and when the battery finally starts to get low, I don't bother to charge it, figuring if my phone is dead, the temptation will be gone. But even with my phone off, it doesn't stop me from thinking about him on a constant loop.

Tuesday comes and goes. Wednesday. Thursday. On Friday afternoon, there's a knock on my door.

I haven't charged my phone in days so I'm assuming it's going to be Fox here to rip me a new one for making him worry. When I open my door I'm surprised to find River standing on my doorstep with concern in his eyes.

"What the hell, Easton?" he blurts as soon as his gaze lands on me, going from worried to pissed off in seconds. "I've been trying to call you for days. I was worried."

My stomach twists. He was worried about me? Of course, he was. We said we were friends, and then I ghosted him without an explanation. With all the crying jags he's witnessed from me he probably thought I offed myself.

"My phone died, and I've been working so I forgot to charge it."

He blows out a harsh breath. "Is this typical? Am I going to be having a heart attack every other week wondering if you're gathering flies? Because, I've gotta be honest, I don't think my heart is strong enough to take that." He puts a hand over his chest and takes a few deep breaths.

"Are you okay?" I ask, worry creeping up. Is there something wrong with his heart? With Paul's heart? Is he going to keel over and leave me mourning another loss?

"I'm fine, just being dramatic." He waves me off, crowding me until I step aside to let him in. "Seriously though, is this something I should get used to from you?"

It's on the tip of my tongue to tell him that he won't have to get used to it because I can't spend any more time with him. But with him standing right in front of me, his cheeks still slightly pink with his outrage, his breathing a little fast, his eyes blazing, I can't bring myself to say it. So what if we had a moment at dinner? I'm sure it was more me than him. I'm still not even sure that he's gay. It didn't mean anything; I was confused and vulnerable, that was all. We can be friends.

"No, I was just in a weird place this week."

River stops and looks at me, his eyes seeming to caress me as he checks for any sign of external injury. "Are you okay?"

I want to tell him no, to say that whatever that moment was between us shook me and made me question everything. I want to tell him that I haven't been able to stop thinking about him for days, and that I feel so guilty about it I've made myself sick. I want to tell him I'm all messed up inside and that it's better if we don't spend any more time together.

But I don't say any of that.

"I'm fine."

He continues to study me, clearly not convinced. "Where's your happy place?" River asks.

The question surprises me, and out of habit, Paul's name forms on my lips, the first answer on my mind. But instead of blurting it out, I force myself to take a second to think about it.

"I used to volunteer to do landscaping for the local humane society. I'd spend all day planting flowers and tending the garden to make the place look nice, and afterward I'd be sweaty, filthy, and tired. The drive home was these back roads, and I'd roll the windows down and crank up my favorite playlist. I always thought it had to be the purest form of joy that could possibly exist."

River smiles. "Show me?"

"What?" I blink at him, not understanding.

"Show me. Take me on a drive."

"Okay."

A slow smile spreads over his lips and it's one of the most beautiful things I've ever seen. I grab my keys and slip on my shoes, and we go out to my car. I feel a little silly as I start the car, trying to decide where to go.

"Take me to that road, your favorite back road that makes you happy," he prompts.

"There's not much to see; it's just farmland and trees."

"I'm not looking for a sightseeing tour. I just want to go somewhere that makes you happy."

His words settle in my chest and make my throat tight. I nod because I know if I try to talk, I might end up crying.

As we leave the city behind us, I roll down my window to let the cool evening air blow around us, and River does the same.

"Wait, we need music," he insists, reaching for my radio.

"Here," I grab my phone and quickly pull up my favorite playlist. A steady, acoustic beat plays from the speakers, and it's the damnedest thing, but when we reach the back road I always drove home from the shelter, it feels like a physical weight lifts off me.

Out of the corner of my eye, River starts to bob his head to the beat of the song, and when the chorus starts to play, he attempts to sing along, even though it's clear he doesn't know the song. He stumbles over words, guessing at some and simply mumbling others, but singing each one with utter confidence that makes a laugh bubble from my chest.

I turn my head to look over at him, and he smiles widely at me, singing even louder and seeming to care even less about getting the lyrics right, now just shouting random words with similar sounds, and I laugh even harder.

One song transitions into the next and, this time, I join him in singing along at the top of my lungs. Flying down the road, the sun setting on the horizon, the car filled with our off-key song, I'm not the man whose husband died tragically, I'm just a guy on a drive with a friend. And I think I might actually be a little happy.

I don't pay attention to how long we drive, but eventually the silliness winds down, and a quieter happiness settles over me. The music reaches into a place in my soul that's been untouched for years and settles me. River's quiet beside me, but his presence gives me a steady sort of peace. It's a transcendent feeling I almost can't put words to, but it almost feels like a rebirth, a fresh start. It feels like maybe things really can get better without Paul. Maybe my life isn't over after all.

It's fully dark by the time we pull back into my driveway. We both get out of the car without a word, and I turn to look at River over the hood of the car.

"Thank you for that."

"It's what friends are for," he says easily. "Try not to worry me like that again, okay? I'm happy to take a drive any time you want, but I don't need any more sleepless nights wondering if you're okay."

His concern wraps around me like a hug, and I feel the barest smile on my lips as I give one short nod. "I'll see you later, River."

"See you later, Easton."

CHAPTER 9

Easton

I pull a package of ground chicken out of the refrigerator, feeling more than a little lackluster about it. Setting it on the counter, I turn and look out the window toward the backyard. My ugly, dead garden still mocking me. *I should replant it*, I think for what has to be the hundredth time at this point. It feels like too big of a task, as overwhelming as it is necessary.

I sigh and turn away from the window, reaching for my phone without thinking about it, and dialing River's number.

"Easton," he says my name with a level of excitement I'm not sure I understand, but it feels nice all the same.

"Hey, Riv. I'm sure you're probably busy, but I'm making dinner, and I was wondering if you wanted to come over and eat with me?"

"That sounds great. I was just leaving the office and trying to decide what I was going to do for dinner. I'll be over in twenty minutes."

"Great."

We hang up, and I tidy up while I wait for River to show up. When I pass the extra bedroom, full of Paul's things, I stop and stand in the doorway. Some days I swear I can feel Paul in the room, his presence filling every corner just like all the boxes of his things. But right now, the only thing I see in this room is a bunch of stuff gathering dust and not doing anyone any good.

Paul would've hated knowing I'd turned my office into a shrine to his things. He would've hated a lot of things about the way I've handled his death. But, if I'm being honest with myself, I think he really would've liked River.

A knock at the door announces River's arrival, and I push myself away from the sad, dusty room and go to let him in.

I open the door, and he steps inside, dressed in a suit like he always is for work. I don't know what it is about River in a suit, but no one should be allowed to be that hot. I feel guilty for even thinking it, but I'd have to be blind not to see how well he wears those damn suits.

"Hey," he says, coming in for a hug. I stiffen in his arms.

"Shit, sorry, that was super weird," he apologizes, releasing me quickly. "I thought maybe we were hugging friends, but I totally made it weird."

"No," I say, reaching out and touching his arm, still able to feel his arms around me from the brief hug. Aside from Fox, it's been a long time since I've felt that. And Fox is basically my brother at this point, so it's nowhere near the same. "It was fine; I just wasn't expecting it."

"So, what's for dinner?"

"I was about to start making chicken meatballs to have with this spaghetti squash I picked up."

"That sounds amazing."

He takes off his shoes and suit jacket, hanging it on the coat rack by the front door. He unbuttons the sleeves of his dress shirt and rolls each one up. What is it about forearms that is so damn sexy? And what the hell is wrong with me that I keep thinking about how hot River is?

He follows me to the kitchen and tells me about his day while I make the meatballs. I'm wrist deep in raw chicken when my nose starts to itch.

"Damn," I mutter, doing my best to use my shoulder to scratch it.

"Here, let me get it," River offers, setting down the knife he was using to chop vegetables for our side dish and coming around the counter.

I close my eyes and turn my face up, offering him my nose. He scratches it gently, and I sigh with relief. He stops scratching, but I don't feel him move away. He's still close enough for me to feel the heat from his body and smell the scent of his deodorant. I let my eyes flutter open, and I realize he's closer than I expected, only a few inches away, looking at me intently with desire and maybe a little fear in his eyes.

I lick my lips and for just a second, I let myself wonder what it would be like to kiss someone who isn't Paul. What it would be like to kiss River. Would he be a gentle kisser? Or would he be all tongue and rough hands? A shiver of wanting runs up my spine, and I find myself swaying toward him, licking my lips.

The oven beeps to alert me that it's preheated, and I jump back, coming to my senses as my heart hammers hard against my ribs. I almost kissed River...*again.*

"It looks like you're done with the vegetables," I say to change the subject. "Want to keep watching the anime we started last time you were over?"

"Sounds good," he agrees, taking a step back, a hint of reluctance in his eyes.

"Go sit down in the living room. I'll meet you in there once I put the meatballs in the oven."

He nods and leaves the kitchen, and I let out a relieved breath. More than anything, I need a few seconds by myself to get my head on straight. I take my time forming each meatball and putting it on the pan to go into the oven, reminding myself that it's okay if I find River attractive, but that doesn't mean it would ever be right to act on it. *Not that I even know that River is gay*, I remind myself again. He hasn't once mentioned a significant other.

Once I get the food in the oven, I wash my hands and head to the living room to find River on the couch, with the next episode of *The Dragon*

Prince ready to start. It feels oddly domestic, and it causes a small flutter in the pit of my stomach.

The couch is small enough that our shoulders brush as we sit side by side. The warmth of his body touches me and seems to surround me, staying right on the edge of my awareness while we watch the show.

"You want to hear something totally embarrassing?" River offers, darting a look at me out of the corner of his eye, a blush rising on his cheeks as he darts his tongue out to lick his lips.

"Of course," I say with a laugh.

"I first got into watching anime in college, and then I discovered bara, and it basically became a major obsession. I even drew some."

My mouth falls open, and my heart beats a little faster, my skin heating up. Bara is popular in Japan, basically anime depicting same sex couplings, and they can be absolutely filthy. I guess that answers my question about his sexuality. Knowing he's into men, at least to some degree has my skin feeling a few sizes too small, my face growing hot. A silly little crush on him when he might've been straight was one thing, but is it wrong now that I know there's a possibility he could feel the same way? I know that should make it better, but it just makes it that much scarier. In a world where things were different, where River didn't have Paul's heart, it's easy to imagine falling for him, *really* falling. But it's too complicated with the connection we share, isn't it?

I push the confused feelings down and angle my body toward him, desperately interested in hearing more.

"Wait, why is that embarrassing?" I ask.

"You don't think spending a ridiculous amount of time drawing porn is embarrassing?"

"Only if it was badly drawn," I reason, and he laughs.

"It wasn't bad. I certainly practiced enough."

"That's amazing. Would it be way too weird if I asked to see some?"

"I don't have them anymore," he says. "I was dating this woman for a while and when she found them it kind of freaked her out, so I tossed them. It didn't take me long to realize that I didn't want to be with anyone who couldn't accept that I'm bisexual, but by then I'd already gotten rid of all my old drawings."

"That's a shame."

"It is," he agrees.

"Fun fact, bara is also the Japanese word for wild rose," I tell him.

"It is? I never knew that."

I nod and give him a small smile. "By the way, when I was a teenager, I totally used to draw my own porn too," I confess, and we both burst out laughing.

When dinner is ready, I dish us up a couple of plates and bring them to the living room so we can watch another couple of episodes. When we finish, I get up to put away the leftovers, and River follows me into the kitchen to help clean up.

"Do you take lunch to work?" I ask as I start filling a couple of Tupperware containers.

"It depends," he says. "Usually I go out and grab something for lunch, but I take leftovers if I have them."

"You can take one of these tomorrow if you want," I offer.

River stops in the process of wiping down the counter to stare at me. His gaze feels heavy, and I can't tell by the look in his eyes what it means.

"I would love that," he says after a few seconds, his voice a little raspy. He clears his throat and starts cleaning again.

I send him home with a container of leftovers and the promise of hanging out again soon. When we hug goodbye, it's a lot less awkward than the hug hello. I think we can definitely get the hang of hugging each other.

River

There's something about knowing I have a container of leftovers special from Easton for lunch that makes me feel warm and fuzzy all morning. I know it doesn't mean anything other than that he had a lot of extra food and didn't want to eat it all himself. But it feels nice to have a home cooked meal from someone. I can't help but think how good it would feel to have someone lovingly pack me a lunch every day, maybe add a little love note to it. I know that sounds cheesy as hell, but I think it would be nice.

"Ready to go to lunch?" Brandon asks just after noon.

"I actually brought lunch today."

"You never bring lunch," he says, narrowing his eyes at me suspiciously.

I shrug and keep my face as blank as possible, afraid if I so much as blink, it's going to give me away. I know Brandon already suspects something is going on between Easton and me, but I'm sure he thinks it's more of a fling than an embarrassingly schmoopy crush.

Brandon keeps studying me, and I squirm under his gaze, struggling to hold onto my poker face. But the longer he looks at me, the harder it becomes.

"Easton gave me leftovers after dinner last night," I blurt out the confession, and my friend smiles smugly.

"That's adorable. This guy your boyfriend or what?"

"No," I scoff. "We're friends; I told you that."

"Dude, *we're* friends, and I'm sure as hell not cooking you dinner and sending you to work the next day with a cute little container of leftovers."

"He's not my boyfriend," I say again.

"Can I ask you a question?"

I sigh. "Please don't let it be about my sex life."

"You haven't dated a man before," he says matter of factly.

"No," I agree.

"Why not?" he asks. "I mean, you're bi, so why not date a guy? Especially when you're crushing on one this hard."

"Reasons," I mutter, not wanting to get into it with Brandon. Easton has his own reasons not to be interested, but those are separate from my own hang ups.

"What reasons? Are you afraid to look gay or something?"

"Of course not. I don't give a shit about that."

"What then?" he presses.

"When it comes to being with a man, I'm a complete virgin. Do you know how embarrassing that is? I'm thirty years old; you really think any dude is going to want to go on a date with me and hear me say 'can we please take things slow? I'm a delicate, virginal flower'?"

"I think you're overthinking it."

I shrug again. "If the right guy comes along then fine, but otherwise I'm perfectly fine the way things are."

"No, you're not," my best friend argues. "And I think the right guy has already come along. Don't miss your chance just because you're afraid."

"What are you, a fortune cookie?" I grumble.

"I got a lot of sleep last night so I'm feeling

really smart today."

"Clearly," I deadpan. "I appreciate it Bran, but it's more complicated than you realize."

"I don't think it is."

After that he leaves to go get his own lunch, leaving me with my leftovers from Easton. I chew slowly, thinking about Brandon's words. Am I holding myself back out of fear?

CHAPTER 10

River

"Hello?" I ask half asleep, early morning sun peeking through my blinds.

"Shit, I woke you," Easton says from the other end of the phone.

"What time is it?" I ask with a yawn, my body coming awake at the sound of his voice, my morning erection especially aware of the man I've spent countless nights dreaming of.

Three weeks after I showed up at his house and we went on a drive, my crush on him has grown with each night spent watching anime on his couch, every container of leftovers sent home for lunch, each Sunday at the art fair, each drive on a quiet back road singing the wrong lyrics and learning all about this man whose smile I can't stop thinking about.

"It's eight," he answers.

"Why are you calling so early on a Saturday?" I complain, stretching my arms over my head to work out the kinks in my shoulders and back.

"I do this art class at the community center on Saturday mornings for kids, and the woman who usually helps me out just called to tell me she's sick and can't make it."

"You want me to come help?" I ask, sitting up and rubbing my face with my free hand.

"You don't have to if you have anything better to do," he hurries to assure me.

"I don't have anything going on. But I've never taught an art class or anything," I hedge.

"It's eight to ten-year-olds so it's mostly just having an extra set of hands."

"Okay, yeah, what time do I have to be there?"

"Can you be here in an hour?"

"You got it."

We hang up, and I throw off the covers and get out of bed.

Forty minutes later I'm pulling up outside the community center freshly showered and bearing tea for Easton. As soon as I get out of my car I wonder if the tea is too much? Is it tantamount to handing him a note telling him I like him? Or am I overthinking things again like Brandon said?

"River," I hear Easton call, and I turn to find him walking toward me from farther down the parking lot. He's lugging a large bin that seems to be too heavy for him, so I hurry over to take it from him.

"Trade you," I offer, holding up the tea.

"You brought me tea?" he asks with surprise.

I shrug, trying not to make a big deal out of

it, even if the little dimple forming on his cheek from the smile he's fighting makes me all kinds of fluttery and happy with myself.

Easton sets the bin down, and I hold the tea out for him. I watch as he takes the first sip and makes a cute little noise in the back of his throat that makes my chest ache.

"Good?" I check.

"It's exactly how I like it," he says. "Thank you."

I pick up the bin off the ground, and it's a little heavy, but not anything I can't handle.

"Thanks. I have to bring my own supplies and depending on what we're working on for the month, sometimes it's a little heavy to carry it all."

"I don't mind," I assure him, following him into the building and down the hall to the classroom we'll be using.

Easton

I can't believe River brought me tea. Not just tea, but perfect tea. No one except for Paul ever got it right. Right after Paul's death, I couldn't drink tea at all for over a year because no one could ever get it exactly perfect the way he did. But somehow River did.

I peek at him out of the corner of my eye as he sets out the small canvases I brought at every station. I can't help but notice the way his t-shirt is stretched around his arm muscles today. Is the t-shirt too small or does he spend a lot of time working out so that his muscles have outgrown the shirt? My heart beats a little faster, heat pooling between my legs and in the pit of my stomach like it did the night at the restaurant.

He mentioned an ex-girlfriend, but I haven't been able to stop wondering whether he's seeing anyone now. If there's a woman...or a man...he spends his time with, who makes him smile and sends him to work with better lunches than I do.

Not that it matters.

The kids start to filter in, and River stands off to the side while I give the main lesson for the day, talking about different kinds of paint brushes for different textures and a *very* beginners tutorial on blending. Then, I turn the kids loose to do some painting on their own and try out the different things I talked about while we make our way around the room to answer questions and offer help where needed.

I keep him in my peripheral vision as I work my way around, my stomach fluttering as I watch him with the kids. He's patient, taking the time to show a few kids the proper way to hold the paintbrushes when they do it wrong, complimenting the blobs of paint they're splashing onto the canvas without care.

"Wow, now I remember why I prefer digital drawing," he says, approaching me with a large, red paint splotch on the front of his shirt.

"Oh no." I jump up, looking around for a rag

or something to use to wipe off his shirt. "I'm so sorry. I'll pay for your shirt," I assure him, ready to rush to the bathroom to grab some damp paper towels since we don't have a rag in here.

"Easton," he says, grabbing my arm to stop me from running off. "It's no big deal. I'll go wipe it off in the bathroom and just throw this shirt out later. It's just a shirt."

"Are you sure? I feel bad."

"I'm sure."

Looking into his eyes, his hand still on my arm, I get lost for a few seconds, unable to look away, and he seems to be having the same problem. My heart pounds hard inside my chest, goosebumps forming along my arms.

"Mr. Harrison?" One of the kids calls, and I blink, taking a step out of River's grasp.

"Coming," I say, giving River a tight smile and scurrying away.

I keep busy helping students the rest of the class, and when it's over, and all the kids file out, picked up by their parents and taken home, the silence feels deafening.

"That was wild," River says, helping me gather up dirty brushes and clean up the room.

"Yeah, it's a little crazy, but really fun."

"It was. If you ever need help again, I'd love to tag along."

"Even at the risk of more ruined shirts?" I ask, cringing again at his red stained t-shirt.

"It's a risk I'm willing to take," he says with a

chuckle.

There's no class in this room on Sundays, which means I'm able to leave the canvases to dry and come back for them tomorrow. Even with the bin considerably lighter, River still insists on carrying it to my car for me. I open the trunk, and he puts it in, then turns back to face me.

He smiles, lifting his hand up to my face and running his thumb along my cheek. Electricity seems to spark where he touches me, my skin humming at the feeling, my whole body becoming a livewire. I'm torn between leaning into the touch and pulling away, my head and my heart at war over the decision.

"Paint," he says simply as he pulls back with a blue smear on the pad of his thumb.

"Oh, right," I reply breathlessly, licking my lips and taking a step back.

"What are you doing tomorrow?" he asks.

"It's Sunday, so I assumed going to the River-walk with you to see the art fair."

"Let me take you somewhere else?"

"Where?"

The corner of his lip quirks with a smile. "Let me surprise you."

"Okay," I agree, my heart beating faster.

"Okay," he echoes, his smile widening before he pulls me in for a hug. I'm starting to get used to it, starting to like it and look forward to it, the feeling of his arms around me, his chest against mine, the warmth of him even through all our layers of clothes.

"I'll pick you up tomorrow morning," he says.

"I'll see you then."

CHAPTER 11

Easton

I'm not sure what to expect when River knocks on my door the next morning. He pulls me into a hug like he always does, and my body tingles from the contact, making me feel giddy and guilty at the same time.

When we pull into the parking lot for the botanical gardens I sit up excitedly in my seat.

"This is where we're going?"

"Yeah, you love flowers, I thought this would be a perfect Sunday outing," he explains a little sheepishly. It shouldn't surprise me that River noticed my love of flowers, but it does. It strikes me how much attention he's been paying—knowing how I like my tea, noticing I love flowers...it makes me feel *special*. Without thinking, I reach out and put my hand over his, the warmth of his skin heating me on contact, making my heart beat a little faster. I swallow around my suddenly dry throat and offer him a small smile.

"Thank you."

"You don't have to thank me. I thought this might be a good place for you to find some of the color you've been missing so much. Call it a selfish move from a huge fan who misses your colors as much as you do." He gives me wry half smile.

"Well, thank you all the same."

We climb out of the car and head for the entrance of the garden. It's still early, so there aren't many people here as we enter. The sound of birds singing fills the air, and the flutter of butterflies make the entire place look enchanted.

We stroll leisurely, taking our time, stopping to appreciate the bursting colors of different kinds of flowers and the welcome shade of the trees lining the walking path. Bumble bees buzz by lazily, not the least bit worried by our presence. The colors make my fingers itch for a colored pencil for the first time since Paul's death and, just like River's hug, it makes me feel excited and terrible all at once.

"I love these. I used to have some in my garden," I say, stopping in front of a patch of calla lilies.

"Have you thought any more about replanting your garden?"

I swallow and lick my lips, my eyes fixed on the pretty white flowers, rippling in the slight breeze. "Yes, I've thought about it a lot lately," I admit.

"And?"

"I'm not sure I'm ready." I look away from the flowers and right at River whose eyes grow sad for a moment.

"It's a big step," he says. "You shouldn't rush

into it before you feel ready."

I nod, knowing he's speaking of more than my garden—just like I was.

"I want to be ready," I admit, almost feeling bad saying the words out loud. "And I think if Paul was here, he'd tell me I need to get on with it already, but it's hard to let go."

River takes a step closer, slipping his hand around mine, lacing our fingers together and giving my hand a light, comforting squeeze.

"Whenever you *are* ready, you're not erasing what you had with Paul, you're just opening the next chapter."

I nod and squeeze his hand in return.

When he drops my hand, the urge to reach out and take it again surges through me. I stuff my hands into my pockets to resist the impulse, and we move on to the next part of the garden, stopping to admire a Koi pond with water lilies floating on the surface. It's soothing to watch the orange and white speckled fish dart around.

"How did you and Paul meet?" River asks conversationally.

I snort a laugh. "I was drunk off my ass in a gay bar, and I spotted him with a few other guys, Fox being one of them, and I absolutely *had* to have him. So, I pushed my way into his group of friends, planted myself right in front of him, and told him I thought he was hot, and he should buy me a drink."

River chuckles. "Wow, that's bold."

"Yeah," I agree wistfully. "I used to be like that—ballsy, feisty, kind of a pain in the ass."

"And it obviously worked," he guesses.

"Of course—I was irresistible," I joke. "I think he thought I was a total weirdo at first, but as the night wore on, we started having a lot of fun dancing and getting to know each other. He came home with me and basically never left." Longing makes my chest ache and my eyes burn. I drag in a deep breath and let it out shakily.

"I'm sorry. I shouldn't have brought him up."

"No, it's okay. I like talking about him; it's just hard. I keep waiting for it to get easier, but it never does."

"I'm sorry," River says again, putting his arm around my shoulder in a friendly gesture. I lean close to him and put my head on his shoulder, soaking in the comfort he's offering, his citrus scent wafting around me, doing funny things to my stomach.

"Have you ever been in love?" I ask.

"I thought I was a few times, but the way you sound when you talk about Paul, I don't think I've felt anything that comes anywhere near that," he admits.

"Just wait, there's someone out there who will make your heart beat faster and your brain work slower, someone who will feel like your true other half, and you'll wonder how you ever lived without that person once you meet them." A flicker of jealousy for whoever that person is heats up inside me. The thought of Paul's heart loving someone else makes me irrationally angry, but it's so much more than that. Thinking about someone else being on the receiving end of all of River's thoughtful attention and sweet smiles is more upsetting than it should be.

I can't decipher the intense look in River's eyes, but his arm around my shoulder tightens, and then he leans forward and presses a gentle kiss to my temple and a ripple of longing races along my skin.

"That sounds wonderful," he murmurs before taking his arm off my shoulder and giving me an apologetic smile.

River

Watching Easton's eyes light up with his dimpled smile as we walk from one end of the botanical garden to the next is more than worth the price of admission. My lips are still tingling from the feeling of pressing against his head. It was crossing the line without a doubt, but Easton didn't protest.

My heart and mind are locked in battle as we walk around, enjoying the morning. Every time Easton talks about Paul, it's obvious how much he still loves him, how far he is from being ready to move on. But then there are the other moments when we get caught up in each other for a few slow heartbeats, both of us unable to turn away. First at the restaurant a few weeks ago, and then yesterday during his art class, among many other moments over the past several weeks. I want him fiercely, and I get the feeling he wants me too.

My heart is pushing me to tell him how I'm feeling, to admit to him that I've been too much of a coward to let myself fall for a man until now, even though I've known I was bisexual most of my life, but I'm falling for him. But my brain keeps insisting that things are great just the way they are, and if I tell Easton how I feel, it will more than likely scare him away.

"You're awfully quiet," he says as we finish the long loop of the massive garden, getting close to the exit.

"Just enjoying all the flowers," I lie.

"It's really beautiful here," he agrees. "We should make this a regular thing; I'd love to come again soon."

"It's a date," I say before I can think twice about the wording, cringing as soon as it leaves my mouth. Easton's step stutters, and he darts a glance over at me shyly, his cheeks turning slightly pink.

"It's a date," he agrees quietly, barely above a whisper, and my heart does a somersault. I'm not falling for him; I've already fallen, and I don't think there's any way to right myself, not that I'd want to if I could.

The entire drive back to Easton's my internal battle continues, made worse by the content smile curving his lips and the quiet way he sings along with every song that comes on.

I pull into his driveway, and the click of his seatbelt being unbuckled seems to echo in the car.

"Thanks again for today; this was great," he says, angling his body toward me and smiling even bigger, the dimple in his cheek deepening. My heart is beating so fast I'm sure I'm seconds away from heart failure, my sweaty hands tightening on the steering wheel as I offer him a smile in return.

"Are you okay? You look like you're going to be sick." He reaches over and brushes a hand against my forehead, and even that brief contact sends jolts through my body.

"I like you," I blurt out, my heart beating so hard I'm afraid it might jump right out of my chest.

"I like you too, River," he says sweetly, putting a friendly hand on mine and smiling at me.

"No, you don't understand." I turn my hand over so we're palm to palm, and I lace our fingers together, meeting his gaze and holding it until I'm sure he can see every part of my soul through my eyes. "All I ever wanted is for someone to make me feel so crazy I can't think straight around them, to spin me around and turn me inside out with a simple look. I like you, and I think I may be falling for you."

His eyes go wide, his fingers gripping mine more tightly. "Oh, River," he breathes out my name in a whisper.

He licks his lips, and I can't take another second of not knowing what they taste like, what they would feel like against mine, so I lean in, closing the space between us. His breath fans over my lips, his eyelids lowering to half-mast as he waits to see what's going to happen next. I'm not sure if I'm giving him time to push me away or simply savoring the anticipation—probably a little of both.

Easton makes a frustrated noise in the back of his throat, his nose brushing against mine before our lips are pressed together. Fully, firmly, irrevocably, I'm kissing a man, and my heart starts to soar. I drag my hands through his hair, grasping his head to pull him closer as our mouths move in tandem. There are no tongues, no groping hands or rutting bodies, like in my dreams; it's simply our lips learning the feel of each other and somehow, it's the hottest kiss I've had in my life.

When my lips part to deepen the kiss, the salty taste of tears finds its way into my mouth, and I pull back to find wet tracks down Easton's blushing cheeks.

"Oh god, I'm sorry, should I not have done that?" I pull my hands away, my gut twisting with guilt at how much pleasure I took from a kiss he clearly didn't want.

"No, it's not you," he assures me, reaching for my hand again and linking our fingers. "It's... it's complicated."

"I'm the first person you've kissed since Paul?" I guess.

"Yes," he admits. "But, it's more than that."

"Tell me?"

A sad smile crosses his lips, and he lifts his free hand to my face, cupping my jaw and dragging his thumb along my cheek. "God help me, I *do* want you." His words almost seem more for himself than for me, but they light a desperate longing in the pit of my stomach.

"You can have me," I whisper, turning my head and pressing a kiss to the pad of his thumb. "Whatever is so complicated it can't be more important than the way you make me feel. Tell me you feel it too."

"I shouldn't, but I do," he admits.

"Then kiss me again," I say with a hint of desperation. I know he'll always love his late husband; I *love* that he loves him, but maybe one day he could love me too. "Please?"

"Dammit, River," he groans, crashing his mouth back into mine.

This kiss is nothing like the first one—there's nothing sweet or exploratory about it as his hand moves to the back of my neck, holding me firmly as his tongue pushes past my lips. I groan as he fills my mouth, kissing me hard and deep until I'm so hot I'm sure I'll burst into flames. My cock is hard and straining in the confines of my pants as I drag my tongue against his, finding the rhythm of the kiss. I slip my hands under the hem of Easton's shirt, feeling his warm skin against my palms, the tickle of his body hair thrilling and brain-meltingly hot.

Desperate to feel more of him, I wrap my arms around his waist and pull him across the center console into my lap so he's straddling me. The horn honks, and we laugh against each other's lips, the moment tasting of nothing but pure joy and possibility. His weight presses against my aching erection, and I can feel the answering bulge in his jeans. I run my hands up his back, over his broad shoulders, and then down to his ass, squeezing the denim clad cheeks and savoring the moan he feeds me.

"River," he murmurs against my lips.

"Mmm," I groan, kissing him deeper, drunk on the taste of his lips, the scratchy feeling of his light stubble against my cheeks, his hard, masculine body in my arms.

"River, stop," he gasps, putting a hand against my chest and pushing me back. "We have to stop."

"I'm sorry, Easton. That was too fast; I know it was, and I'm so sorry."

"Shh." He presses one more gentle kiss against my lips before reaching over and opening the driver door, climbing off my lap and getting out of the car. "I have to think."

"Take all the time you need; I'm not going anywhere," I promise, and his eyes soften.

"You're a really good man, River." He

reaches back into the car and puts his hand over my rapidly beating heart, his eyes fluttering closed and a tear streaking down his cheek. "I'm sorry," he whispers as a second tear falls, following the same path of the first, caressing the gentle curve of his cheek.

"You don't have to be sorry for anything," I assure him.

His eyes flutter open again, and I can see guilt and confusion written there.

"I'll see you later. Drive home safe."

I watch as he walks into his house, and then I sit in his driveway another few minutes, trying to get my racing thoughts and pounding heart under control. I can still taste him on my lips, still feel him in my arms, and I have no idea if the memory of this one kiss will have to be enough to get me through the rest of forever, or if Easton might just give us a chance to see if we can be something more.

"I promise to take good care of him if he lets me," I vow to Paul. I won't pretend to have any idea what happens when we die, but I say it on the off chance he can hear me, wherever he is. My heart gives a small twinge.

CHAPTER 12

Easton

Surprisingly, I didn't cry after River drove away, leaving my body soaring and my lips tingling from the kiss we shared. I didn't cry, but I *did* spend the next few days in a fog of confusion and delicate hope, trying to imagine what it might be like to have a life with someone who isn't Paul, to wake up every morning beside him and plan a future, and whisper in the dark about all the things we want to do together along with promises of forever. The thought makes my heart ache with yearning and guilt.

And I spend a lot of time thinking through the implications of our other biggest obstacle: River's heart, Paul's Heart. Can I let myself fall for River without telling him the truth? If he knows the truth, will it shatter this fragile thing we're building right now?

I ask myself all these questions and daydream about a future that's not as lonely as the last five years have been. I draw my black and white and shades of gray novel while eyeing my untouched colored pencils. I wake up every morning to an empty bed and itch to call River and tell him how much I want to take a leap and see where this might lead.

Then, Thursday rolls around. Not just any Thursday. It's June fifteenth, which makes it six years since I lost Paul.

As soon as I wake up, it's like I can feel the weight of this particular date blanketing and suffocating me. I reach for Paul's cold side of the bed, dragging his pillow to me and burying my face in it. But unlike all the years past, I don't cry. My heart aches, and my soul feels fractured, but the little flower of hope River seems to have planted in me over the past couple of months is like a little flower growing through the crack, keeping the unending despair at bay.

Out of habit, I reach for my phone to call Fox, to share the sadness of this day with Paul's oldest and best friend, but at the last second, I dial River's number instead.

"Easton?" he answers with restrained excitement that brings a smile to my lips.

"Hey, are you on your way to work already?" I ask.

"Not yet, why?"

"Do you want to get coffee?" I ask, and then realize how silly that sounds since neither of us actually drink coffee. "Or whatever," I add, self-consciously.

"Or whatever," he agrees with a chuckle. "Do you want to meet at Cool Beans?"

"Sounds good. I'll see you soon."

River looks delicious as always in his tailored suit, leaning against the outside of the coffee shop with a smile. The memory of our kiss five days ago has my blood heating and my heart beating faster. As much thought as I've given it since Sunday, I still don't know what the right thing to do is. And maybe today isn't the day to make any life altering decisions.

I stop in front of River, and his eyes turn warm, just like his smile. He opens his arms, and without a second thought, I fold myself into them, pressing my face into his chest and breathing him in as his arms go around me, wrapping me in a fierce hug. I press myself into him much longer than the acceptable length of time for a friendly hug, but he doesn't seem to mind, and the contact does my fragile soul a world of good.

When I finally pull back, I tilt my head back to meet his gaze, and River lifts one hand up to cup my jaw, running his thumb gently over my cheek, gathering moisture I didn't realize was there.

"Easton—"

"River—" We say at the same time and then both laugh.

I step back out of his grasp entirely and take a breath before looking into his eyes again.

"I'm not done thinking about things—I just...needed to see you today."

"Okay," he says easily, not seeming to feel impatient or annoyed. "Let's get not-coffee then and maybe a couple of pastries," he suggests with a smirk, and I nod, following him into the coffee shop.

We place our order and grab a table. River watches me over the rim of his cup as he lifts it to his lips and takes a sip.

"So, what are you up to today?" he asks conversationally after he sets his cup back down.

"I was thinking about buying a new bed," I say, surprising myself. I hadn't considered buying a new bed, at least not consciously. I'm not sure what might happen with River, but whether it's River or someone else years down the line, I'm not going to bring another man into the same bed I shared with Paul. Besides, it's past time I got a new one—springs have been poking me in the back, and one of those memory foam ones seems like it would be nice.

Even without me saying it, the sympathy in River's eyes suggests he understands the subtext. He gives me a sympathetic nod and reaches across the table to put his hand on mine.

"If you think it's time."

"It's the anniversary of his death," I blurt.

"Oh, Easton, I'm so sorry."

"It's okay." I wave him off, taking a sip of my hot tea and looking around the coffee shop aimlessly. "Sometimes I can't understand how time could just keep ticking on without him. It seems so wrong that the world itself didn't end that day."

"It did go on though. Your life went on and so did the rest of the world. All I know about Paul is what you've told me, but I can't imagine he'd have wanted your life to end when his did."

"He wouldn't have," I agree. "He would've liked you."

"That means a lot to hear."

I nod again and take another sip of tea, my knee bouncing under the table. "It's not as hard this year as it was the last five. I don't know if it's because time really is making it easier or if it's…" I trail off, catching River's eye and feeling a blush creep into my cheeks.

"If me being in your life is helping at all, then I'm glad to hear that." He lifts my hand to his lips and presses a soft kiss to my knuckles before releasing it.

"Thank you."

"It's funny, today is my six-year anniversary of getting my new heart too. I bet we were in the hospital at the exact same time," he muses, and my stomach twists. This is my opening. If I'm going to come clean, this is the perfect chance. But I can't force the words past my lips. I can't bring myself to tell him the truth.

"You stopped for coffee without telling me," a voice from behind me says, and River smiles.

"Sorry dude," he replies with a shrug, and I turn to see the same man who was in the pictures Fox gave me. "Easton, this is Brandon. Brandon, Easton." He does the introductions, and I reach out to shake his hand.

"Nice to meet you," I offer.

"You too. You've been monopolizing my best friend lately, but since I've never seen him smile this much in my life, I guess I can let it slide," he jokes, and I can feel myself blushing.

"All right, we'd better get to work," River announces, jumping up from his seat.

"Wait, I want to hear more about how happy our friendship has made you," I tease, and River's cheeks turn bright pink.

"Next time," Brandon offers with a wink, letting River shove him toward the door, and they both disappear.

Almost as soon as they're gone, my phone starts to ring, and I already know who it is before I even look at the display.

"Hey, Fox," I answer.

"How are you holding up?"

"Honestly?" I take a sip of my tea, slumping back in my chair. "A little better than usual."

Fox is quiet for a few seconds. "Because you're still seeing River?" he guesses.

"I think so," I admit even as the guilt of it creeps up my throat and tries to choke me. "He makes me feel better. He makes me want to *want* to get better."

Fox goes quiet again, for longer this time until I can't take waiting any longer.

"Just say it," I sigh.

"What?"

"I can hear you judging me, so just say it already."

"Nothing. I was just wondering if this is healthy or not."

"I'm fine," I grumble. I pull my phone away from my ear, intent on hanging up when a new thought occurs to me. Maybe Fox *wasn't* just calling to judge me and make me feel guilty. Maybe he was calling because today's a hard day for him too. Because I wasn't the only person who loved Paul. I wasn't the only one who lost him that day.

"How are *you* holding up?" I ask.

"It's hard," he admits. "It's always hard. Every day is hard, but you know how today is. It feels like yesterday."

"I know."

"I miss him," he admits.

"I know," I say again, wishing Fox was here so I could give him a hug.

River

"You are in deep smit with that man," Brandon says as soon as we're outside.

"Deep what?" I ask with a laugh.

"Smit," he repeats. "You're totally smitten with him."

"I am not," I mumble, feeling my cheeks heat again.

"Oh, whatever. I have *never* seen you look at anyone like that before. You were like a real-life heart eyed emoji."

"Whatever." I shake my head and bite my lip.

"So, what's the deal anyway? You guys still pretending you're just friends or what?"

We walk into the lobby of our building and get on the elevator. I hit the button for our floor and wait until the door closes before I answer.

"I kissed him."

"What?" It's almost comical how wide Brandon's eyes go at my admission. "When? How was it?"

I groan, wishing I hadn't opened this can of worms, while at the same time, desperate to tell *someone* about the incredible, life altering kiss.

The doors ding open on our floor, and Brandon follows me to my office, shutting the door behind him and plopping himself down in the chair in front of my desk.

"Tell me everything, right now."

"Oh my god, you are such a gossip queen," I complain.

"Call me whatever you want—just spill the details."

"There's not much to tell," I lie. "On Sunday we hung out, and I kissed him."

"Where?" he asks, leaning forward with interest.

"On the lips?"

My best friend bursts out with a laugh. "Good to know, but I meant *where*. Were you on the couch watching a movie and you just went for it, or what?"

"In my car. I don't know what came over me, but I just blurted out having feelings for him, and then I kissed him."

"Nice." He nods approvingly. "How was it? He's the first guy you've kissed, right?"

"It was..." My mind drifts back to the feeling of Easton's lips moving against mine, soft and sweet as we explored. The memory of tracing the curve of his bottom lip with the tip of my tongue is seared in my mind, heating me up from the inside out.

"I'm guessing it was good, based on the look on your face right now," Brandon chuckles.

"It was amazing," I agree. "But, um, he kind of cried after."

"He *cried*?" he repeats. "Are you really that bad of a kisser?"

"No, asshole. He hasn't kissed anyone since his husband died."

"*Oh*. Wow, that's heavy, dude."

"Yeah," I agree.

"So, is he looking for some kind of rebound to get back in the saddle now or what?"

"I don't know. He said he needed to think, so I'm not pushing it."

"What about you? Is this just an experiment on the gay side of your sexuality to break you out of your rut?"

"Easton isn't an experiment," I snap, and Brandon holds his hands up defensively.

"Just checking."

"I..." I clear my throat and shift in my seat. "I really like him."

"I can tell," he says. "I just don't want to see you get hurt."

"I'll be fine," I assure him.

"I hope things work out. Easton would be lucky to have you."

"Aw, you big sap," I tease, smirking at my friend.

"Shut up." He laughs, picking up a pen and chucking it at me before getting up and leaving my office.

God knows where things might go with Easton, but I've never wanted anything more in my life.

CHAPTER 13

Easton

I shift in my bed, looking up at the ceiling and trying to decide if I like it or not. It felt comfortable in the store, but now that it's here in my bedroom, it's almost *too* comfortable. It's unsettling. The sheets feel all wrong too. I figured if I was getting a new bed, new sheets just made sense, but these don't smell the same, don't feel the same. I'll never be able to sleep in here.

I sigh and roll off the bed. Hopefully, when it's time to actually sleep, I'll be tired enough that the strange new bed won't bother me as much. For now, I need to start on dinner before River gets here.

Even with a few additional days to think things over, I still haven't made a decision about that kiss and what it meant, what I *want* it to mean. But that didn't stop me from inviting River over for our usual Saturday night dinner and anime hang out. He's given me space all week to think, and I hate to admit it, but I miss the hell out of him.

I glance over at the framed picture of Paul and me on our wedding day, sitting on the top of my dresser.

"What do I do?" I ask the still photograph of my smiling husband. "I don't know what's fair to you, or to River...or to me, if I'm being honest. I wish I knew the right thing to do."

Of course, I don't get any kind of answer, just the quiet of my bedroom echoing around me as my plea for guidance hangs in the air. When I give up waiting for some sort of sign from Paul or the universe or whatever higher power might be out there, I shuffle to the kitchen and start on dinner.

By the time River knocks at the front door, I'm pulling the eggplant parmesan out of the oven.

I open the door to let him in, and he greets me with a sheepish smile and a hug. He has his computer bag with him for the first time since he showed me some of his work the first time we hung out. He clutches the strap as he toes off his shoes, and rather than setting it down, he keeps it with him as he follows me to the kitchen.

"It smells amazing in here."

"Eggplant parmesan—I hope you like it."

"Mmmm, I definitely do," River says, sniffing the air shamelessly.

"You can set your computer bag down if you want."

"Oh, right." he blushes and puts his bag down.

"Did you bring something for me to look at?"

His blush deepens, and he dips his head to

avoid my gaze. "Maybe, let me see how brave I'm feeling after dinner."

I chuckle, grabbing a couple of plates to dish up our food. "Fair enough," I agree.

River goes to the bathroom to wash his hands and then sits down at the table. When I set his plate down in front of him, he licks his lips, and the memory of how they tasted against mine heats my body from head to toe. I absently reach for my lips, tracing the bottom one with my index finger just like his tongue did, and I shiver, my cock starting to harden in the confines of my jeans.

He looks up at me with a sweet smile. "Thank you. You've been spoiling me with all these delicious meals."

"It's more fun to cook for someone else," I say with a shrug, not letting him see how much it means to know he likes my cooking.

"Did you end up getting a new bed?" River asks once I sit down with my own plate of food. His tone is casual but slightly strained like he's working hard to make it that way.

"I did; it was delivered today," I answer. "I'm not sure if I like it. It's not what I'm used to."

He nods, taking a bite of his food and chewing it slowly. "It can be difficult to get used to something new."

"Maybe it's worth it though?" I add cautiously, my heart beating faster as I play his game of trying to sound casual. "In a few weeks, it might be the best bed I've ever had."

"You don't know unless you try it out."

"Yeah."

He holds my gaze for several long seconds before we both return to eating, and the conversation turns to lighter subjects for the rest of the meal.

"I'll do the dishes," River offers as soon as we're finished eating.

"You don't have to do that."

"You cooked, so it's only fair," he insists, picking up both our plates and taking them to the sink.

"At least let me dry." I join him as he fills the sink with warm water and soap, submerging all the dishes. There's something painfully domestic about the moment, our shoulders brushing as we work side by side. River starts to whistle a tune, and I feel myself smiling, my heart feeling lighter by the second. He hands me a clean, wet plate, and I turn my head and brush a kiss to his shoulder before taking it and drying it. His smile widens, but he doesn't call out the gesture, doesn't press to know what it means, and I'm grateful for that.

"So, do you want to show me something?" I ask once we're finished with the dishes. River's eyebrows scrunch in confusion, and I laugh, nodding toward his computer bag.

"Oh, right." He bites down on his bottom lip and shifts on his feet.

"I'm not going to be mean about it," I assure him. "I was nice before, wasn't I?"

"Yeah, it's not that," he says. "It's…" He blows out a breath and goes to pick up his bag. "Come on, let's sit down, and I'll show you."

We get comfortable on the couch, and he pulls out his Tablet and hands it to me. I notice a slight tremble in his hand as he holds it out, just before I take it. I don't think he was this nervous the first time he showed me his work.

I lean back and pull my legs up to curl them underneath me and start to read the first panel. The first thing that strikes me is that it's in black and white like my own graphic novels, which is a change from the work he showed me before, and as I read, something inside me starts to unfurl. The story is about a god who falls in love with a mortal from afar and starts to grant him wishes. When the mortal wishes the world was more beautiful, that's when River starts to draw in color. It starts small, roses in the background, a single butterfly, but before long everything is vibrant and breathtaking, and the mortal is utterly in love with the color, even not knowing it was made for him alone.

I don't realize I'm crying until a tear falls onto the screen. I sniffle and look up at River to find him watching me intently, chewing his bottom lip again and still as a statue.

"What do you think?" he asks cautiously.

"You wrote this for me?" I already know the answer, but I need to hear him say it. Flowers are blooming more vibrantly than ever from the cracks in my soul.

"Yes," he answers, his voice husky. I set the computer down on the coffee table and turn to face him on the couch.

"You want to give me my colors back." This one isn't a question at all; I can see it written all over his face.

"Yes," he says again, shifting closer to me so I can feel the heat of his body. "I know I could never replace Paul, but if you let me, I think I could help color in your world again."

"You already have." I cup his face between my hands, and when our lips meet, my entire body feels like a livewire.

River's arms go around my waist, and I moan into his mouth as he pulls me closer, his lips parting so I can deepen the kiss. Our mouths move hungrily against each other, my hands slipping into his short, soft hair as I lean back and take him with me until his body is blanketing mine.

He drags his lips away from mine, kissing along my jaw and down to my throat, nibbling and licking my skin.

"I'm so crazy about you, Easton. I've never felt this way about anyone," he confesses, and a small sob escapes my chest. I arch my body to get closer to his, tilting my head so he has better access to my neck.

"You're incredible, River. I shouldn't want you, but you've made it impossible not to. I want you so badly I can hardly think of anything else."

He works his way back up to my lips, his hands slipping under my shirt, his fingers ghosting over my stomach and chest. I can feel the hard ridge of his erection pressed against my thigh, and I moan, grinding myself against it as my own cock grows harder.

I drag my hands from his hair and run them over his biceps and up to his shoulder blades. I've always had a thing for a strong set of shoulder blades, someplace to dig my fingers into while I'm getting fucked. I moan out loud at the thought. It's been *so* long since anyone has touched me like this. I didn't think I'd ever *want* someone to touch me like this again, but River's hands on me are like rain after a drought.

His tongue sweeps into my mouth, and I press my fingers into his shoulders. Our chests heave against each other, and I swear I can feel his heart thundering against mine, finding the same rhythm and beating as one. Instead of making me sad, this thought fills me to bursting with joy and hope.

It's been a long while since I dated much, but I can say with certainty, I've never met a man as content with kissing as River seems to be. He doesn't make a move to unbutton my pants or undress me. He doesn't seem in any kind of hurry to move things along, and I find myself just as content to simply kiss him, learning the shape of his mouth and memorizing his taste.

I let my hands roam over his back, down to

his firm, round ass to give it a little squeeze that makes him moan into my mouth. We kiss until my lips feel numb and swollen, and my face feels rubbed raw from his stubble. Then, he rolls us over so he's underneath, and I'm resting on top of him as he continues to run his hands gently over my body.

"Is this real?" he asks, his voice a harsh whisper. I wiggle up his body and press our foreheads together.

"I can't promise I'm going to be a picnic as a boyfriend, but I want you, River. I want to see where this leads."

"Boyfriends?" he repeats, his eyes sparkling.

"Let's try."

He cups my jaw and presses a soft kiss to my lips. "Boyfriends," he says again with wonder.

"Have you, um…have you had a boyfriend before?"

The shy look is back in his eyes. "Not technically, no."

"So, you've just fooled around with guys?"

"Not technically, no," he says again with a laugh.

"Wait, you *have* been with a man, right?"

"No, I haven't," he admits. "I've known I was bi since I was a teenager, but I've never really explored it."

A smile spreads across my kiss bruised lips. "Was I your first kiss with a man?"

"Yes."

I don't know why, but that makes me feel all mushy inside.

"Thank you for giving me something so special." I bump my nose against his and kiss the corner of his lips.

"You don't think it's lame? I'm basically a thirty-year-old virgin when it comes to this stuff."

"It's not lame, it's sweet, and I would be honored to be your first...everything," I tell him, brushing his messy curls off his forehead. "Let's take things slow, okay? There's no need to rush anything."

"Okay," he agrees.

We lay like that for hours, talking late into the night with his arms around me and my head on his chest. When he finally decides it's time to leave, I go to the kitchen to grab his leftovers, and on a whim, I grab a slip of paper and write a sweet little note that I tuck into the bag along with his lunch. I hope it'll make him smile when he finds it.

I'm so tired, once he's gone that I collapse into bed and fall asleep with a smile on my lips, dreams of River filling my thoughts.

CHAPTER 14

River

On my way to work on Monday morning, I swing by a flower shop and place an order to have a bouquet of colorful wildflowers delivered to Easton. On the card I write, *Here's a little color like I promised you until you can find your own.* I debate whether to put *Love, River* or just *River* as the sign off. It's probably a little soon for the *love* bit, but that doesn't stop my heart from leaping in my chest at the thought of it. I settle for simply *River,* and the florist gives me a big smile.

"You've got a very lucky young lady," she says.

"Man," I correct. Her smile doesn't falter, and I let out a small, relieved breath, realizing I just came out for the first time to a stranger. Hell, my mom doesn't even know. I suppose I should tell her, since I *do* have a *boyfriend* now. Just thinking the word makes me feel a little giddy.

It's a struggle to focus most of the morning, but not in the morose way it is at times. I watch my phone, waiting for Easton to call once the flowers are delivered. I hope it wasn't too much to send flowers. As the morning drags on, doubts creep in, and I start to worry he was just swept up in things last night and woke up regretting it this morning. Maybe it was too much too soon.

When my cell finally rings just before noon, I nearly crack the screen, hitting *accept* so fast on the call.

"I can't believe you sent me flowers," he says, but the tone of his voice sounds pleased, so I smile to myself.

"Do you like them?"

"They're beautiful. They really brighten up my kitchen."

"Good, I'm glad," I say. "Are you free tonight, I want to take you on a proper first date."

Easton sighs, but the sound is happy. "I'm free for a date."

"Great. I'll pick you up at six thirty."

"I'll see you then," he agrees, but doesn't hang up right away. We both linger, not saying anything but not wanting to hang up. "I dreamt of you last night," he confesses after a few moments of loaded silence.

"Oh?" I breathe out the word as my body heats. "What'd you dream?"

"Mmm, I'd better wait until later to tell you; it's a bit indecent to say over the phone," he purrs out teasingly, and I groan.

"I guess I'll tell you about my dreams later too, then. They're certainly more than a little indecent."

"I'm looking forward to hearing about

them."

"I'll see you later, Easton."

"See you later," he agrees, finally hanging up. I reach down to adjust my rising erection, leaning back in my chair with a smile on my lips, my heart beating fast and heavy, and my stomach twisting itself in excited knots.

When Brandon comes to grab me for lunch, I spill my guts to him about my new boyfriend status with Easton, and I'm entirely sure I sound like a thirteen-year-old-girl, and I have absolutely no shame about that.

I open my lunch and find a note along with the leftovers Easton packed. *Kissing you is the most fun I've had in ages. I can't wait to do it again soon.*

Brandon ribs me about how hard I'm blushing before I tuck the note into my pocket for safe keeping and dig into my lunch.

The afternoon moves just as slowly as the morning did, and when five o'clock finally arrives, I'm already halfway out the door.

I head home to shower and change, my body buzzing excitedly the entire time. I ignore my erection as I wash up and push thoughts of Easton joining me in the shower out of my head as best I can. I whistle to myself as I shave, and when I'm finally dressed and ready to pick up Easton, I can't get to his place fast enough.

As soon as Easton answers his door, I pull him into my arms and kiss him. His hands go to my chest, fisting the fabric of my shirt to steady himself, his body melting into me, his lips going soft and pliant under mine. When I pull back, his eyes stay closed for several seconds, his grasp on my shirt not loosening immediately, as if he needs a few moments to come back to himself, before he finally blinks slowly and regains his balance.

"Hi," I say with a smile.

"Hi." The dimple on his left cheek is on full display as he grins up at me, making my heart flip and my stomach flutter.

"Ready to go?" I ask and he nods, stepping outside and pulling the door shut behind him. I put my hand on his lower back to guide him to the car, opening the passenger door for him when we get there.

"Wow, aren't you a gentleman," he teases.

"Get used to it," I say, kissing his cheek before he climbs into the car, taking pleasure in the pinking of his cheeks.

"Where are we going?" Easton asks once I'm in the car as well.

"There's this taco truck downtown that has fish tacos that are to die for, then I thought we'd walk around a bit?" As I say it, it sounds like it's not enough for a first date, not impressive enough.

"That sounds perfect," he says, reaching over and putting his hand over mine. "I know this is totally cheesy, but as long as I'm spending time with you, I'm happy."

"Me too."

Easton

River was right, these are hands down the best fish tacos I've ever had. And that includes the ones Paul and I had in Maui on our honeymoon.

"I got kind of distracted yesterday after you showed me the graphic novel you've been working on, but I wanted to tell you, I think my agent would be salivating to get you a contract for it," I tell him as we walk, eating our tacos and enjoying the warm evening.

"You really think so?"

"I do. I can set up a meeting for you, if you want."

River wrinkles his nose. "Does it count if you're the one who gets it for me? It's not really on my own merit or talent, is it?"

"I won't tell him you're my boyfriend or anything," I assure him. "I can just say you're a friend I mentored a little and that I think your work would sell."

"Yeah, okay," he agrees. "What the hell, it can't hurt, right?"

"It can't hurt at all," I agree.

After we finish our tacos, we stop at an ice cream shop that we pass, and if there's anything cuter than the two of us walking down the street hand in hand, each with an ice cream cone, I don't know what it is.

"I came out to the woman at the flower shop today," River says conversationally as we walk.

I squeeze his hand. "God, I keep forgetting that this is new for you. You didn't even hesitate to hold my hand or kiss my cheek right in front of the taco stand."

He shrugs. "It's a little bit of an adjustment, but honestly, it feels so damn good to be open like this for the first time. Not that I *wasn't* being myself when I was out with women, because that's part of who I am too, but this is like a whole different me, getting to experience the world for the first time. Does that make sense?"

"It makes perfect sense. If I'm rushing you with any of this, just tell me. I don't mind keeping the PDA on the down low," I assure him.

"Don't, I like it." He squeezes my hand, and I tilt my head to rest on his shoulder for a few steps.

We walk and talk for hours until it starts to feel chilly, and my feet start to get tired. During the drive home, I dart glances out of the corner of my eye at River, trying to gather the courage to invite him inside once we get there.

I nibble my lip as we pull into my driveway, my heart beating hard and fast, my palms damp with sweat, no matter how many times I wipe them on my jeans. We said we'd take things slow; is it too soon to invite him in? On the other hand, just because I invite him in, doesn't mean we need to go at it like wild animals or anything.

"I had a lot of fun tonight," I tell him as I unbuckle my seatbelt.

"Me too."

"Do you want to come in for a few minutes?" I ask. The expression on River's face is a mixture of excitement and terror, which oddly seems to calm my own nerves. "Come on, I promise I don't bite."

River's eyes smolder at me, and he huffs out a small laugh before turning off the engine and un-buckling his seatbelt as well.

My heart is in my throat as I lead him up to the door, my hands clenched in fists to keep from trembling. I've had River at my house dozens of times in the past few months—there's nothing to be nervous about.

We both slip off our shoes at the door and head into the dark living room. I reach for the lamp beside the couch and turn it on to give the room a warm glow instead of using the harsh overhead lights.

"Do you want anything to drink?" I offer, shifting on my feet.

"I'm good," River says, sitting down on the couch and patting the spot beside him. "Come sit with me. I think we could both use a few seconds of deep breathing," he suggests with a laugh.

I shake my head and smile, sliding onto the couch beside him. "Sorry, I don't know why I'm so nervous. You'd think I'd never been with a man before."

"Well, since *I* haven't, I'm certainly not going to complain about taking things slow." He puts an arm over my shoulders, and I wiggle close to him, running my nose along his smooth cheek. He must've shaved just before our date. I'm not sure why, but that thought makes me smile.

"How slow are we talking?" I ask, my voice coming out huskier than intended.

River turns his head and our noses brush, his lips an inch from mine. Our breath mingles, and I swear my entire body is vibrating with the delicious anticipation of the moment.

"Not *too* slow," he murmurs before capturing my lips with his. I whimper against his mouth and kiss him right back.

Climbing onto his lap, I part my lips and moan as his tongue licks into my mouth. Slipping my hands under his shirt, I run my fingers along his soft stomach. He's not fat by any stretch; I doubt he could be with how carefully he watches his diet, but he's not necessarily muscular either. He feels strangely familiar as I drag my hands up his chest, like coming home somehow. When my fingers brush the rough edges of the scar in the middle of his sternum I freeze, reminded for the first time in over a week of the connection that originally brought us together. It's too late to tell him, and, I'm afraid, too late to turn away from the road we're on.

"Sorry, it's kind of gross, right?" he says, pushing my hand away from his scar.

"No," I say, shaking my head and pulling his shirt over his head. I dip my head and press a kiss to the long, jagged scar. "It's beautiful, just like you."

River's breath hitches, and he slowly burrows his fingers into my hair. He pulls me back to his lips to kiss me again before breaking contact to pull my shirt off too. Our bare chests press together with our next kiss, the rhythm of our lips and tongues growing more heated as our hands grope and explore each other. The hard bulge of River's arousal is pressed firmly between my legs, a moan falling from his lips into mine with every thrust of my hips.

I reach between us and fumble with the button on his jeans, my cock aching, precum soaking the inside of my boxers as I grind against him, making the task of getting his pants open all the more difficult.

I finally manage to get them open, slipping my hand inside and feeling River's pleasure rumble through his chest as I wrap my hand around his hot, silky, steel length. His precum wets my palm when it passes over the head of his cock, slowly stroking him.

"Oh fuck," he moans around my tongue, thrusting his hips up, dragging his cock through the tunnel of my fingers. "I want to touch you too," he mutters, his trembling fingers trying to get my pants open too. I take mercy on him, popping my button with my free hand and freeing my erection.

River pulls his lips from mine and looks down at my exposed cock with a pleased sort of wonder before reaching out and running his finger along the glistening head and making me groan from the tentative contact. He licks his lips, looking into my eyes as he wraps his hand around my length, his expression heating as he feels the weight of another man's erection for the first time.

"Too fast?" I check, still slowly jacking him.

"No." He presses his face into my neck, licking and nibbling at my skin as he tries to match the same rhythm I'm using with his hand on me.

I run my free hand along his chest, the heat of his breath against my throat making my cock throb in his hand. My palm grows slick and sticky from his precum, making it easier to stroke him with each pass. I thrust into his grasp, my gasps and moans growing desperate. I forgot what it felt like to have a hand other than my own touching me, wringing pleasure from me. But more than his hand on my cock, the feeling of a steady, warm body against mine is pushing me to the edge faster than I would've expected.

"So good," River gasps against my Adam's apple, canting his own hips as well. I want more, *need* to feel so much more of him, or I think I might go insane. As if reading my mind, River releases his grasp on my cock and grabs me around the waist, lifting me to lay me flat as he hovers over me. I hurriedly push his pants down around his thighs and do the same to my own, and when he blankets me again with his body, his erection flush with mine, my eyes roll back with pleasure.

"I need it," I moan, digging my fingers into

the taut globes of his ass, encouraging him to thrust against me. River grunts and bucks his hips, humping against me.

"Easton," he groans my name as he ruts against me, my body writhing under his, matching his thrusts with my own as sweat and tears dampen my face. For a change though, they aren't sad tears, far from it.

"So good, oh god," I moan pressing my face against his shoulder as my balls tighten, my fingers digging harder into his flesh, no doubt leaving bruises as I cry out in pleasure, my cock erupting against his, coating us both in my thick, sticky release. Wave after wave rolls over me, taking me out of my own head for a change, lighting up my body in a way I forgot was possible. River's body moving against mine draws out my orgasm until I'm sure it'll go on forever. Tears stream down my face unrestrained as my chest heaves against his.

River lets out a harsh groan, and his release mixes with mine. He thrusts against me until we're both empty and spent, cum and sweat coating our bodies.

It's not until he catches his breath that he notices the tear stains on my cheeks as well.

"Was that okay?" River asks, sitting up and brushing his thumbs along my cheeks.

"It was great. Sorry, I should've warned you, but I have this embarrassing habit of, um, crying when I orgasm," I admit, feeling my face flame. It wasn't that embarrassing with Paul because we'd been together long enough that I'd outgrown feeling self-conscious about it, but before him, it was a bit mortifying to cry during a hookup.

"As long as they're not bad tears."

"Not at all," I assure him. "Come on, let's get cleaned up." I take River's hand and lead him down the hall and through my bedroom to the master bath. He leans against the sink, shirtless with his pants still open, and I have to admit, it's a pretty sight. His lips are puffy, and his hair is sticking up in all directions, a few little love bites standing out on his neck.

I grab a clean rag from the linen closet and run it under the sink before stepping in front of him and using it to clean the cum off his stomach. He watches me with a gentle smile the entire time, tilting my head and kissing my lips when I finish.

"This was the best date I've ever been on," he whispers against my lips.

"Me too," I confess.

CHAPTER 15

River

The smile on my lips is starting to feel like a permanent fixture in the past few weeks since Easton and I started dating. My heartbeat quickens just thinking of him, and I pick up the pace, desperate to get to him faster.

I slow when I near the restaurant we agreed to meet at for dinner, just around the corner from my office, and I spot Easton through the large window. My stomach flutters and everything inside me feels like it's made of helium. He's sitting at a table, a relaxed smile on his lips that I almost can't believe I put there. I've only just started memorizing the taste and curve of his lips, and there's no doubt I'm fully addicted. If he's growing tired of me constantly stealing kisses while he cooks us dinner or turning every movie night into a make-out session as if we were in high school again, he hasn't shown it. Every time I put my hands on his hips or wrap my arms around his middle and pull him in to press a kiss to his lips, he lights up like a Christmas tree.

I can't believe I ever thought I loved anyone before Easton. What I've felt for anyone in the past hasn't come anywhere close to this.

As if he can feel my eyes on him, he glances over and spots me through the window, his smile widening as he tilts his head to gesture me to hurry up and get inside. Heat blossoms in the pit of my stomach, a familiar itch under my skin driving me to get closer to him, to never let Easton go.

My feet carry me to the door and into the restaurant. When I reach Easton, I sweep him out of his chair, holding him against my chest to kiss him breathless, not giving a damn who's watching.

"Hi," he murmurs against my mouth with a hint of amusement.

"Hi," I say back, dragging my lips against his, my hold on him tightening for a second before I reluctantly set him back down.

"So, don't leave me hanging, how'd it go?" Easton asks immediately as I take my seat across the table from him.

As promised, he got me a meeting with his agent, Mark, to discuss representation for my graphic novel. We met for lunch, and I am still buzzing from it.

"He loved it. He thinks he can sell it to a publisher."

Easton makes an excited squealing noise, drawing the attention of people at the surrounding tables, and I chuckle, my chest warming at the happiness radiating from him that was absent only a few months ago when we first met.

"I'm so happy for you and so proud of you,"

he says, reaching across the table to put his hand over mine.

"Are you sure this is on my own merit, not because of my connection to you?" I ask the question that's continued to nag me since he first mentioned setting up the meeting.

"I swear. If anything, your connection to me probably hurt you with Mark. I'm usually a total dick to him; I think he hates me."

I snort a laugh into my glass of water and then reach for my napkin to wipe my face. When I glance back up, I notice someone approaching the table. It's the man I met briefly when Easton and I went for coffee weeks ago. Fox.

I give him a friendly nod in greeting, and Easton turns around to see, his eyes going wide and his body stiffening.

"Fox, what are you doing here?"

"I was too lazy to cook myself dinner, so I thought I'd come get something to eat. I tried to call you to see if you wanted to join me. I guess I know why you didn't answer now," he explains, raising his eyebrows and glancing between the two of us.

"You've met River before," Easton says, clearing his throat and shifting in his seat before he waves toward me.

Fox grunts and nods at me. An awkward silence descends over us as he continues to stand beside the table, not saying anything else. I can see hurt and confusion in his expression, and guilt in

Easton's. I wonder if Easton has been blowing off hanging out with him in favor of spending time with me. The thought doesn't sit well with me.

"Would you like to join us?" I offer.

Fox's gaze flickers between the two of us again, and his jaw ticks.

"Sure, why not," he agrees after a few seconds. Easton shoots him a look that looks like a warning before forcing a smile.

"Great," Easton says through clenched teeth.

There's clearly layers of context here I'm not understanding, so when Easton looks back in my direction, I give him an apologetic look. His lips quirk in an easier smile this time, and he waves me off.

"So, you and Paul were close friends?" I ask Fox and notice him stiffen again, a look of surprise on his face.

"Easton told you about Paul, huh?"

"Of course I told him about my husband," Easton cuts in, giving Fox another of those warning looks.

"Paul and I were best friends since high school. He was one of the best men I've known in my life."

I nod, taking another sip of my water. "What do you do for a living?" I ask next, hoping to find a topic of conversation that isn't painfully uncomfortable. It's obvious the two of them are close, and I understand why Fox might be wary of someone taking Paul's place, but I want to get along with him.

Easton grows still, his face going a little pale.

"I'm a private investigator. I find people, catch cheating spouses, that kind of thing."

"Oh, that must be exciting."

He shrugs. "I like it."

The waitress appears, mercifully saving us from all the awkward. Once we place our orders, I excuse myself to the bathroom to wash my hands.

Easton

"You haven't told him," Fox says as soon as River is out of ear shot.

"Of course I haven't told him," I snap. "How the fuck would I tell him something like that? Please don't say anything."

He raises an eyebrow at me and lets out a slow breath. "What's going on here? I thought you were done spending time with him."

My cheeks heat, and I dip my head to avoid his gaze. "It wasn't that easy," I confess.

"Is this about Paul? You feel like being around River gives you some kind of connection to him?"

"No," I answer quickly. "That's not it at all. Maybe when I first wanted to meet him that was it, but now..." I trail off, my stomach squirming and my heart pounding faster.

"Wow," Fox says with a harsh laugh. "Okay

then."

Before I can ask what he means by that, River returns to the table, and I decide if Fox is ever going to accept what's going on, he needs to get to know River for who he is, just like I did.

The tension eases and conversation becomes more comfortable now that I know Fox isn't going to tell River the truth and ruin everything. Guilt twists my gut, the unspoken lie bitter on the back of my tongue, but I know if it's out there, it won't do any bit of good.

The rest of the meal is slightly less awkward, but not entirely. Fox is polite when he leaves, shaking River's hand and giving me a hug.

"You know what we should do?" River says as soon as we're alone again.

"What's that?"

"The four of us should go out, me, you, Brandon, Fox," he explains. "I'd love for you to get to know Brandon better, and I'd like to get to know Fox better since he's your best friend."

"Fox isn't my best friend, he's Paul's best friend," I argue. He quirks an eyebrow at me. "Fuck, Fox is my best friend," I realize. When the hell did that happen? Not that I don't love Fox. He got me through the rough times and was always a great friend to Paul, it's just that Fox and I don't exactly have a lot in common for him to fall into *best friend* territory.

"After Paul died, I guess I pushed all my other friends away," I say. "I never thought about it until just now. They tried to call and come around a lot at the beginning, trying to cheer me up. But eventually they gave up and left me to my wallowing. Fox was the only one who kept coming around no matter how messed up I was. I guess because he was just as messed up about Paul as I was."

"They can't have been that good of friends if they left you when you needed them most."

I shrug. "I guess not." I look at River and think about all the ways he's made my life better since he came into it—reminding me how to smile again, giving me a reason to be happy. "I think you're my best friend."

His smile widens until he looks like a little kid being presented with a puppy.

"Don't tell Brandon, but I think you might be my best friend too," he admits, putting an arm over my shoulder and kissing the top of my head. "What do you say though, about the four of us hanging out?"

"Let's do it," I agree. "There's this fun bar Fox, Paul, and I used to go to. There's live music a lot and the drinks are good and cheap. As long as Brandon doesn't mind a gay bar?"

"He won't care," River waves it off. "If there's booze, he'll be happy. I didn't realize Fox was gay though. I couldn't really get a vibe one way or the other from him."

"That's probably because he's on the Ace spectrum. Depending on his mood he either says he's fully asexual, homoromantic, or he says he's demisexual."

"Oh, wow. So, does he date?"

I shrug. "Not that he tells me about. I figure it's not really my business."

"Yeah, I just bet he's lonely. You guys were so close after Paul's death, and now you're sort of getting on with your life, I bet that's hard for him."

His words hit me square in the chest. I hadn't thought of it that way, but it makes perfect sense. Paul was Fox's best friend in the world, he lost almost as much as I did when he died, and now I'm blowing him off and ignoring his calls all because I feel guilty about River.

"You're right. I'll do better from now on," I vow. "Thank you."

CHAPTER 16

River

I can't stop re-reading the note I pulled out of my lunch.

I'm thinking of you.

It's simple—four small words—but they speak volumes. Easton is thinking of me. He was thinking of me when he packed these leftovers for me to take for lunch, and he's thinking of me now, in the middle of the day, just like I'm thinking of him.

No one has ever put a note in my lunch before. Hell, no one ever packed me lunch before Easton, and it never fails to make me feel all warm and gooey inside. Everything about Easton seems to make me feel that way.

"Dude, with the heart eyes," Brandon complains, stepping into my office without knocking.

I wad up a napkin and toss it at him. "Jealous."

"I wasn't at first, but I'd be lying if I said you weren't starting to make me a little curious to know what all the fuss is about," he admits with a chuckle.

"About relationships?"

I don't miss his moment of hesitation before he says "yes." And I can't help but wonder about it. He sets his takeout bag on my desk and reaches inside to pull out the contents, eyeing my homemade lunch with obvious envy as he does so.

"Still up for coming out tonight?" I check with him.

I'm hoping like hell that spending time with Fox on purpose, rather than accidentally running into each other, will make it less awkward. At the very least I'll have Brandon as a buffer this time around. I was serious when I told Easton that I wanted us to get to know each other's friends. I know we haven't been together long, but I like the direction things are moving in, and our friends are important to us, which means a good impression is important.

"Of course," Brandon assures me. "I'm looking forward to getting to know your man better."

It's ridiculous how much the phrase *your man* makes my blood heat and my stomach flutter happily. Easton is my man. God, that sounds good.

"For fuck sake with the heart eyes," he complains again, and I give him the finger and a smile.

*****

"Nice place," Brandon says as we pull into Easton's driveway. Since I don't drink, I offered to drive everyone so they could let loose if they want. What better way to get on Fox's good side than to be DD so he can get shit faced if he feels like it?

"It was his and his husband's," I explain, and Brandon lets out a low whistle.

"Dude, I don't think I could stay here if it was me. Does he have a freaky shrine to his husband or what?"

I think about the second bedroom, filled almost wall to wall with boxes of Paul's stuff. "Not a shrine," I answer. "He has his stuff in the extra bedroom."

"That's still rough. Maybe it's just me."

The front door opens, and Easton steps out. My heart immediately starts beating faster, and I'm sure I have heart eyes like Brandon was teasing me about earlier. I unbuckle my seatbelt and jump out so I can greet him, wrapping my arms around Easton's waist and hauling him against me for a kiss. He makes a happy little sound against my lips, and I drink it in, wanting all of his happy sounds, all of his smiles.

"Thank you for the note in my lunch; it made my day," I murmur quietly so Brandon won't hear and mock the shit out of me.

Easton smiles, the dimple on his cheek showing. I brush a kiss against the dimple before releasing him and turning to open the car door for him.

Brandon greets him and the two of them chat casually as I drive to pick up Fox, with Easton directing me.

When he comes outside, I notice a hint of

the usual scowl on his face, but when he reaches us, he does force a smile, so at least he's trying. He greets me with a nod and climbs into the backseat next to Easton.

The bar isn't far, and it's not at all what I expected when we step inside. I've never been to a gay bar, and I'll admit, when Easton mentioned it, I *may* have pictured a bunch of dudes in leather, assless chaps.

"Disappointed?" Easton asks with a hint of humor in his voice as he slips his hand into mine.

"No," I assure him. "It's more low-key than I expected, and I'm completely good with that."

"This isn't really a hookup bar," he explains. "It's more of a hangout. This neighborhood is where most of the older gay couples live."

"How did I never realize that before?"

"Probably not paying attention," he laughs. "Let's get drinks."

We get drinks, alcohol for them and water for me, and grab a table far from the stage so we'll still be able to talk once the live music starts. I pull out Easton's chair for him and kiss his cheek as he sits down, loving the way his skin goes warm with a blush as I do so. I can feel Fox's eyes on me, and when I look up, I notice they're softer than I've seen them before. If treating Easton right is the way into Fox's good graces, I'm more than up to that challenge.

Fox and Brandon get along better than I expected, seeming to find numerous things in common to talk about. The drinks keep coming and Easton becomes more handsy by the minute, practically climbing into my lap at one point. Not that I'm complaining.

Easton

With Brandon and Fox deep in conversation, and the alcohol making my head feel fuzzy and my chest light, I lean over close to River and brush my lips to his ear as I whisper, "Meet me in the bathroom in two minutes."

His breath hitches, and he raises an eyebrow at me. I slip a hand under his shirt, dragging my finger suggestively along the waistline of his jeans. The same jeans that have been hugging his ass perfectly and driving me insane all night long. Flicking my tongue against the shell of his ear, a thrill runs through me. I missed adventurous, flirty Easton; it was always one of my favorite colors.

River gives an almost imperceptible nod, and I smile before stepping away as casually as I can manage and sauntering to the bathroom. Sparks of heat dance along my skin, my cock hard as steel and my throat aching to be filled with River's cock.

When we said we'd take it slow, I meant it. I haven't been in any rush to check every box just for the sake of doing it. There's been something almost achingly sweet about the anticipation of what might come next. And I've come to have a whole new appreciation for dry humping, if I'm honest. It's erotic in a way I never considered when the main goal was always oral or anal with past hookups. And, of course, with Paul we were together long enough that we had sort of a standard playlist that I guess I took for granted after a while.

The door to the bathroom opens cautiously, and River peeks inside to find me leaning against the sink waiting for him.

"Lock the door," I tell him as he steps inside.

I notice a slight tremble in his hand as he does as I say before turning back toward me.

I push off the sink and cross the distance between us, pushing his back against the door and devouring his mouth. He grunts in surprise, and I can feel his lips curving into a smile under mine before he parts them, and his tongue sweeps into my mouth. River's hands find their way to my ass, squeezing it through the rough denim of my jeans and holding me against him, our erections crushed together between us.

"I want to go down on you," I murmur against his lips, slipping both hands under his shirt and feeling him shiver under my touch, his stomach muscles contracting as goosebumps pebble his skin.

"Here?" he asks breathlessly.

"It feels exciting," I confess, taking his hand and putting it over my heart so he can feel how hard it's pounding. "I feel like I'm going to come out of my skin, and I want to take you with me," I laugh.

River tucks his face against my throat, taking a deep inhale against my skin and then darting his tongue out to flick against my Adam's apple. "Yes, please."

I groan at the feeling of his lips moving against my throat as he agrees. My hips jerk forward, pressing against the shape of his arousal and letting it light a flame in the pit of my stomach. Then, I take his face between my hands and kiss him again, our tongues tangling in a hungry, inelegant sort of way as I work his jeans open and then slip my hand inside to wrap around his erection.

River moans against my lips, bucking into my grasp. His cock is hot and smooth in my fist, hard enough to pound nails and practically pulsing with arousal. Precum slicks my palm as I slide my hand over him. Lust thunders in my veins making it almost hard to breathe as I stroke him, pressing myself against him as fully as I can as we kiss, wishing there was some way to meld with him, become one with him, be fully absorbed into River.

I wrench my lips away from his and drop to my knees. Looking up at him from this position sends another jolt of excitement through me. I'm on my knees in the bathroom of a bar, River's pants around his thighs, his thick cock inches from my face. It's filthy and exhilarating. It's something old Easton would've done, and it feels fucking incredible.

With my fingers wrapped around the base of his cock, I angle it toward my lips, parting them only half an inch, not enough to take him inside. River's chocolate brown eyes are wild as he looks down at me, his cheeks stained red and his chest heaving. His own lips are parted and damp from our kiss. I lock eyes with him as I drag the tip of his cock over my bottom lip, glossing it with his pre-cum and feeling him throb in my grasp.

"Jesus, Easton," he groans loudly.

"Shh, someone could be right outside," I warn, dragging the head of his cock over my upper lip this time and then darting my tongue out to gather the salty flavor of him.

He lets out a frustrated huff, biting down on his lip to keep himself quiet. I open my mouth wider and lave my tongue fully over the head of his cock, swirling it and then dipping the tip into his slit in search of more of his flavor.

"Oh fuck," he whimpers as I slowly start to stroke his shaft at the same time. I love the feeling of his skin moving with my grasp, bunching and stretching over his stiff length.

A thicker drop of precum beads at his slit and I lap that up greedily, watching as River's eyes roll back, his fingers tunneling through my hair, his legs tensing.

Wrapping my lips around his crown, another groan whooshes from his lips, his grip on my hair tightening. I continue to use my tongue as I suck, my hand still working him, our gazes locked. It's been so long since I've had a cock in my mouth, but apparently it's like riding a bike because as soon as the solid weight of his erection rests against my tongue, I crave it like a hit of fucking heroin. I slurp him down, my own cock impossibly hard and fucking throbbing in my pants as he hits the back of my throat.

I hum at the feeling of him filling my mouth, relaxing my throat and taking him deeper until his balls are pressed against my chin, and my nose is buried in his pubes. His hands are in my hair and shaking, his fingers clenching and releasing as his hips twitch involuntarily.

I pull back and drag in a ragged breath before grabbing his hips and pulling them forward, encouraging him to thrust, to fuck my mouth like he wants to. His eyes go wide, sounds of pleasure tumbling from his lips as he takes me up on my offer. He thrusts gently at first like he's afraid of giving me too much or hurting me. I dig my fingers into the round globes of his ass cheeks and pull him harder, slamming his hips into my face while I hold his gaze so he can see the flare of heat in my eyes as his cock goes down my throat again.

"Oh god, oh god, oh god," he chants as he fucks my face, drool running down my chin, hastily drawn breaths burning my lungs each time he pulls out before plunging back in.

I whimper and moan around his length, shoving a hand into my pants to fist my painfully hard cock. I jerk myself with the same punishing pace River ruts into my mouth, heat pooling in my stomach and starting to spread up my spine.

River tries and fails to muffle his own moans, and I couldn't give less of a shit if someone hears us. Hell, the whole club could have ears pressed to the door for all I care. His cock thickens between my lips, and his thrusts stutter. I hum encouragingly around him, sucking harder and being rewarded by a loud curse from River's lips and the salty flood of his release down the back of my throat. He presses himself flush against my face, his cock as deep as possible in my throat as it pulses out his orgasm, his whole body twitching as he gasps my name and tugs my hair until it stings.

I let out a muffled cry around his cock stuffed in my mouth as my own orgasm rolls over me, coating my fingers as I jerk myself in earnest, splattering my cum onto my jeans and the bathroom floor without a care.

"Holy fuck," River sighs, easing his softening cock out of my mouth and letting me draw in a much needed lungful of oxygen.

"Damn, you're wild," I rasp out, my throat raw from the pounding it took. I lick my lips, tasting remnants of his release still lingering there.

"Sorry, was that too rough?" he asks, concern filling his eyes as he tucks himself away.

"I liked it," I assure him, holding out my clean hand so he can help me up. I wash my cum covered hand off in the sink and then zip myself up while River washes his hands as well.

The wild lust between us has simmered leaving the same sweet, simmering affection that's become a staple the past few weeks. He opens his arms, and I step into them, resting my head against his shoulder and sinking into the hug.

"What color do you think public sex is?" I ask, and he chuckles.

"That was crimson, without a doubt."

"I like crimson," I mutter against his shoulder before turning my face and pressing a kiss to his neck.

"Me too."

He finally releases me, and I stumble a little as I step out of his grasp.

"Shit, I think I'm more drunk than I realized," I laugh.

"Fuck, should I feel bad about what just happened?" Guilt colors his previously relaxed expression.

"Don't you dare."

I slip my hand into River's, and we head back to the table. Fox gives me a knowing look as I slip into my seat and I shrug, unashamed as I reach for my drink and take a sip.

"We thought you guys took off," Brandon says, and even in the dim light of the bar, I notice River blushing a little.

"Not yet," I say, cutting a look at River and smiling at him over my drink. He reaches under the table and puts a hand on my thigh. I lean into his touch and smile as my heart settles into a happy rhythm.

We stay a little longer before we all decide we're old and it's time to call it a night. We pile back into River's car, and he drops off Fox and then Brandon before heading toward my house. A happy buzz from the alcohol and the bathroom tryst keeps a smile on my lips, where I can still taste River.

"I think that went well tonight," he says as he pulls into my driveway.

"I think it went better than well," I flirt.

"Well doesn't even begin to cover how *that* went," he agrees. "But I mean with Fox and Brandon. Do you think he's warming up to me at all?" River asks with a hint of insecurity. I want to tell him Fox's frostiness has nothing to do with him and everything to do with me. But then I'd have to explain things I'm nowhere near ready to explain.

"He'll come around."

"You think?"

"Of course," I assure him. "How could anyone not like you? You're the sweetest man alive."

I unbuckle my seatbelt and lean over the center console to brush a kiss to his lips. I almost want to invite him in but it's too much, too soon, so I don't. I kiss him until I can't tell if it's the booze or lack of oxygen making me dizzy and then I stumble up to my front door and let myself inside. River waits in my driveway until I'm all the way in and my living room light is turned on, then I finally hear him pull away.

CHAPTER 17

Easton

I pull on my gardening gloves like armor for battle, staring down the plot of weeds and thorny branches left from long dead rose bushes. I'm ready to tear up the tangled, dead mass of my life and replace it with something new. It's time. It's *long* past time.

With trowel in hand, I march across the backyard to my garden, dropping to my knees in the soft dirt, and grabbing a handful of the infiltrative plants and yanking. They come up, roots and all, mangled in my fist and strangely cathartic.

I toss the handful over my shoulder and grab for another, tearing it mercilessly from the ground. I can't believe I let the weeds get so out of hand, I can't believe I let them destroy the garden I worked so hard to tend for so many years. Paul would be so disappointed in me. He'd tell me I've been mourning him too long and letting my life slip away. It's long past time I pulled out all the dead things in the garden and let it live again.

Sweat and tears mingle on my face as I furiously pull up more and more weeds, grabbing at the dead rose bushes and trying to pull those out as well. When the bush doesn't budge, I use my trowel to unceremoniously hack at the soil, exposing all the roots as I breath heavily, entirely too emotional. But for once the tears running down my cheeks don't feel heavy, they feel cleansing. I'm bleeding out my grief and throwing it away with the dead plants and weeds.

When the rose bush is loose, I grab it again to pull it out, the thorns leaving deep scratches on my arms that don't slow me in the least. Little beads of blood form along my arms, and I start in on digging up the roots of another bush.

By the time I yank up the last weed and toss it on the large pile, my arms and back are aching, my eyes are burning from sweat and tears, and my soul feels light.

"East?" Fox's voice has me whipping my head around. I find him standing on the porch watching me with a combination of surprise and worry.

"Just clearing out the garden," I explain, wiping my arm, covered in blood and dirt, across my forehead.

"You're...you're going to replant it?"

"Yeah, I thought some azaleas might be nice, maybe a lavender bush so the yard will smell nice," I explain. "Probably no more roses," I add wryly, holding up my arms to show him the battle scars.

He stares at me a few more seconds like he's seeing me for the first time in years. Maybe he is. I don't know who's been living in my skin these past five years, but it certainly hasn't been me.

"That sounds great."

"What are you doing here anyway?"

"I was worried when you weren't answering your phone, so I thought I'd swing by."

"I'm fine," I assure him. "Better than I've been in a long time, actually."

"I can see that," he agrees. It looks like he wants to say more but he doesn't, he just looks at me with curious eyes until I can't take it anymore.

"Want to help me burn this stuff?" I ask, gesturing to the pile of dead plants.

"Sure." He steps off the porch and helps me transport the pile into our former fire pit. I used to love having bonfires on warm summer nights, sitting back here with Paul and Fox, drinking beer late into the night as the fire crackled. It's just another thing I lost when Paul died.

I wonder if River likes bonfires.

Once the fire pit is piled high with the corpses of my dead garden, we set it on fire. Strangely, the smoke is as cleansing as the tears were.

"Did you have fun when we went out the other night?" I ask as we stand and watch the dead plants burn. "What do you think of River?" I ask, tugging my bottom lip between my teeth, almost afraid to hear his answer.

"Honestly?" He cuts a look in my direction, and I shift on my feet.

"Yes."

"I think he seems like a good guy," he admits. "I get why you like him."

A relieved smile spreads across my lips. "Yeah?"

"Yeah," he says. "And, I think you need to tell him the truth," he adds as we watch the flames dance and pop.

"I can't," I argue, shaking my head. "It's too late, plus, he might think it's the only reason I want to be with him."

"Is it?" he questions. "Is falling into a relationship with River your way of hanging onto Paul?"

"No." I don't feel the need to elaborate or defend myself, and Fox doesn't say anything else.

We watch the flames turn the remnants of my old garden to ashes, and then I go inside to take a shower. Just before I turn on the water, I hear Fox's car pull away, and I wonder what he thinks of me, what Paul would think of me finally moving on to be with someone new.

I step under the hot spray and watch as the water turns muddy around my feet before being washed down the drain. I scrub the dirt and blood from my skin, the sorrow and death. I wash it all away.

River

Easton greets me with a hug when he opens the door, and the first thing I notice are angry red scratches all over his forearms. Grabbing his hand, I lift his arm to my lips and kiss a few of the offending spots.

"What happened?"

"I'll show you," he offers, tugging me inside and toward the back of the house. We step out onto the back porch, and the scent of fire hangs heavy in the air. And then I notice the garden, no longer overgrown, now a patch of freshly tilled dirt that looks ready for planting.

"You pulled out all the weeds and dead rose bushes."

"It was time," he says simple. "Past time, honestly."

It's more than a gardening project. I know what the dead garden meant to Easton, why he waited so long to tend to it. My chest feels too tight for the swelling of my heart as I wrap my arms around Easton's waist from behind, stooping to rest my chin on his shoulder, and turning my face to press a kiss to the side of his neck.

"I'm proud of you. I know that wasn't easy."

He leans his weight back against me, and I'm more than happy just to hold him for as long as he's content to stand here. Nothing has ever felt more right than Easton in my arms, and the fact that he finally felt ready to tear up the dead garden has so much hope blooming in my heart.

"Will you help me plant a new one?"

"You want me to help? I thought this was your thing?" I've never gardened before, but I'll give it a shot if it's what he wants.

"I think it would be fun to have your help, to look out the kitchen window in the morning when I drink my tea and know we brought the garden back to life together."

There's no doubt how significant this gesture is. His garden is his heart, and he wants me to have a hand in making it beautiful again. For Easton this is tantamount to asking me to adopt a dog together. It's permanent and important to him.

"I'd love to help," I say, kissing his temple. "I can't get in the dirt because of the risk of toxoplasmosis or a fungal infection, but I'll help in whatever way I can."

"Is it hard having restrictions you always have to remember?"

I shrug. "I'm used to it."

"Do you want to start now?" he suggests. "We can go to the garden center and pick what we want to plant. We don't have to finish today."

"I can't think of a better way to spend a Saturday," I tell him honestly.

On our way to the garden center, I roll down all the windows in my car so we can enjoy the warm early summer morning and crank up the radio for us to sing along to. Easton's smile is easy now as he tilts his head back against the headrest and lets his eyes fall shut with a content look on his face.

"You're the most beautiful man I've ever

laid eyes on," I tell him just to see the blush on his cheeks and the dimple that appears as his smile widens.

"Flatterer," he accuses, and I chuckle.

"It's true. The first time I laid eyes on you my heart started beating so fast I could hardly breathe."

"That's because you'd nearly been hit by a bus; the adrenaline was kicking in," he teases.

"It was because my heart was trying to beat out of my chest to get closer to you," I correct, and I notice him stiffen for a moment, the flash of a frown marring his features so quickly I almost missed it before he fixes a smile back in place.

The garden center is busy this morning as we pull into the parking lot and find a space to park.

"What are your favorite kinds of flowers?" Easton asks after we grab a couple of carts and add a few bags of nutrient rich dirt to one of them.

"I've never given it much thought. Is it lame to say daisies?"

"Not at all. Let's get some daisies." he says, grabbing a few trays of daisies we can plant along with a few packets of seeds. "This way we can have some now and be sure that more grow next year," he explains.

He does the same with a few other flowers, notably skipping the roses.

"No roses this time?"

"I think I'm done with roses for now," he

agrees with a dramatic shudder.

As we load the purchases into my car a little while later, I take note of the bursts of color, and it fills me up inside. I want Easton to have every shade of every color painting his life with happiness and love. My heart twinges at the thought, and as I look up to find Easton smiling at the flowers as well, I realize I love him. Not like it's been with anyone else, telling myself I should love them, there was no reason not to love them. No, this isn't love because I should, this is love because there's no way *not* to love him. This love is like breathing. This love has become part of every cell of my body, even in this short amount of time.

"Why are you looking at me so weird?" he asks with a laugh.

Because you just turned my world inside out without even trying, I want to say. *Because I love you so much nothing else makes sense anymore.*

Instead of saying those things, I lean over and capture his lips in a gentle kiss, pressing our foreheads together when our mouths part.

"Let's go add some color to your life," I suggest.

"Let's," he agrees.

By the time we get back to his house and have everything unloaded in the backyard, the sun is starting to heat up the day, and I feel the first trickles of sweat down the back of my neck. Easton hands me a pair of garden gloves and a shovel and we get to work spreading the dirt. I use the shovel while he gets down on his hands and knees and gets up to his elbows in it.

I can see why he enjoys this, there's something relaxing about the mindless physicality of it—muscles aching with repetitive movements, sweat dampening my shirt. As we move into planting the flowers, I whip my shirt over my head and toss it out of the way, which helps me cool off a little and also has the added bonus of drawing an appreciative gaze from Easton.

He licks his lips, and my mind travels back to last week at the bar when he went down on me in the bathroom. I've had plenty of blowjobs in my life, but I swear if giving head was an Olympic sport, he would take home the gold easily.

A smile quirks the corner of his lips as if he can read my gutter thoughts from a few feet away. Just in case he can, I throw in a few images of me returning the favor, filling my mouth with him for the first time and making him writhe with pleasure.

"Do you have a gardening fetish?" he teases, his eyes flicking down to the growing tent in the front of my shorts.

"Apparently," I joke. "By the way, you have some dirt on your cheek."

He uses the back of his hand to try to wipe it but only smears more.

"Did I get it?"

"No, come here."

He comes closer, and I pounce, pushing him

onto his back and crawling on top of him while he starts to laugh. Our lips slide together in a messy kiss, our teeth clanking as we both continue to smile.

"Why do I get the feeling that was a set up?"

"There really is dirt on your face," I defend, using my hand to wipe it off before kissing him again. "But I *may* have used it to my advantage so I could get my lips on you."

"You won't hear me complaining."

CHAPTER 18

Easton

Even with all the goofing around we do—and taking a long break for lunch so we could make out and trade handjobs—we still manage to get the garden finished by the time the sun starts to set.

"I don't think I've ever been this sweaty in my life," River says as we head inside.

I eye his bare chest appreciatively, tracking one of the aforementioned sweat droplets as it makes a path from his collarbone, over his pec, and down to this happy trail.

"Want to take a shower?" I offer.

"I probably should."

"Mind if I join you?"

His eyebrows go up, and a smile spreads over his lips. "I thought you'd never ask."

We leave our muddy shoes near the back door and make our way down the hallway to the master bathroom. River's shorts hang low on his hips, his round ass flexing with every step he takes. Feeling playful, I reach out and pinch his ass cheek, eliciting a surprised, squealing laugh from him.

"Dude," he complains, rubbing the spot.

"Sorry, I couldn't resist. If you want, I can kiss it and make it better," I offer suggestively.

"Maybe once I'm not so sweaty."

"Deal."

I start the shower, and we both strip out of our sweaty, dirt covered clothes and toss them into the hamper. It strikes me that this is the first time we've been *completely* naked together, and my stomach does a little flip. Not that we haven't seen and touched each other's fun bits, but totally naked still feels like a new step.

I can feel River's eyes on me before I turn back around. It feels like they're burning me, branding me, everywhere they land, and I love it. My cock is half hard when I face him again and his is the same—plump and heavy between his thighs. I step closer, pressing our bare bodies flush against each other, feeling the weight of his growing erection against mine, and I tilt my head to kiss his lips.

I can taste his salty sweat and the warm sunshine on his mouth. I can taste earth and lust there too as his tongue slips past my lips, his strong hands caressing down my back and cupping my ass cheeks.

Steam starts to fill the bathroom, and I pull away, giving River a playful smile before I slip out of his grasp and into the shower. He follows me, pulling the curtain closed behind him, making it feel like we're in a world all our own here. I used to love taking showers with Paul, reveling in the way he'd take his time washing me, teasing me with hot kisses until I was panting and begging him to give me more. For once, the memory doesn't make me sad. I appreciate it for what it is, a beautiful time in my life with a man I loved with all my heart.

River reaches for the bar of soap on the little ledge and rubs it between his hands to create suds and then starts to run his hands over my shoulders, down my arms and back, and I melt into his touch.

If I loved Paul with all my heart, what will it mean if I let myself love River? Does that mean I can't ever love *him* with all my heart because that already belonged to Paul? Or does the heart have some magical ability to increase its capacity for love at will?

River's soapy hands knead into my muscles, tense from all the hard labor we did today, and I sway toward him.

Even if I don't understand how it would work, I'm afraid I might be falling in love with him anyway.

Fox's words from yesterday worm their way into my mind, the censure in his tone when he said I need to tell River the truth. I don't think he's wrong, but I don't even know how or where to begin. It feels like it's too late to tell him now, but the idea of hiding it from him forever turns my stomach sour.

"You're so tense," he murmurs, massaging my shoulders and leaning close to kiss my neck.

"Mm," I make a noncommittal sound and try to force the issue from my mind for the time being. I'll have to deal with it eventually, but it's not vital at this exact moment with River all wet with his hands all over me.

I pluck the soap from his hands and turn back around to face him, soaping up his body just like he did mine and collecting every one of his contented sighs and pleasured groans to save inside my heart.

After our shower, I'm too worn out to cook so I suggest ordering dinner, which River jumps at.

"I have a serious sushi craving if you're down for that," he says.

"Bring it on," I agree.

We cuddle on the couch, kissing and talking while we wait for our dinner to arrive and then I let him laugh at my lack of chopstick skills as I attempt to eat it.

River

After dinner, I pull Easton onto my lap to kiss him. Our lips play, and my hands roam over his body, slipping under the elastic waist of the sleep pants he put on after the shower. He offered me a pair as well so I wouldn't have to put my dirty clothes back on, and neither of us bothered with underwear.

I can feel the heat of his cock through the

thin layers of fabric between us, my erection rising rapidly as I start to think of all the things I'm more than ready to try with him. He's been true to his word about taking things slow so I could get my bearings, and now I'm looking forward to jumping into something new with both feet.

I knead the taut globes of his ass in my hands, licking my way into his mouth and imagining my tongue on other parts of his body. I want to taste him *everywhere*, feel all the parts of him I haven't yet. I want to find all the ways to drive him out of his mind with pleasure. It may be too soon to tell him that I'm in love with him, but I'd be happy to show him.

"Do you, um…" Easton says, blushing a little as he wiggles on my lap.

"Yes," I answer with humor, completely up for anything he's about to suggest.

He chuckles and runs his hands up and down my chest, his palms grazing my nipples through my shirt and making me shiver.

"Let's go get in bed," he suggests more confidently this time.

Nerves have my pulse jumping, but I follow him as he climbs off my lap and leads me back down the hall.

When we reach the bedroom, he strips his shirt over his head and tosses it on the floor before turning to face me.

"We won't do more than you're comfortable with, but I really want to feel your body against mine," he says, taking a step forward, his eyes trained on mine to gauge my reaction before he grabs the hem of my shirt to take it off as well. I lift my arms, letting him strip me bare in more ways than one.

Our pants go next, hastily shoved down and kicked aside before we climb onto the bed, Easton stretching out beneath me. His skin is hot and smooth as it slides against mine, sparking like kindling everywhere we touch. I've known I was bi since my crush on Leonardo DiCaprio when I was twelve, but I had *no* idea just how good it would feel to have a hard body under mine, coarse hair and sharp lines and the deep rumble of his groans all making my cock swell and ache.

"Can I touch you?" I ask. "I want to explore you and learn all about the ways to light your body up."

Easton moans and arches his back, spreading his legs wide and stretching his arms over his head.

"Do anything you want to me, River. I'm all yours."

His words reach inside me stoke the fires of my lust even higher. I kiss him hard, dragging my hands over his thighs and wrapping them around my waist. Our erections press against each other, hot and firm and familiar after all the times we've gotten off rutting against each other. I didn't expect dry humping could be that enjoyable, but tonight I want to find new ways to experience his

K.M. Neuhold

body.

I pull back from the kiss and sit back on my heels.

"Do you have lube?"

"In the top drawer," he says, pointing at the nightstand. I stretch over and open the drawer, finding a bottle of lube and a small, curved vibrator there. My cock jerks at the thought of Easton getting himself off with the vibrator in his ass, pressed against his prostate. Maybe he'll show me sometime.

I grab the lube and shut the drawer, shuffling back into place between Easton's legs. I may not have been with a man before, but after spending the past few weeks deep in Google research, I feel more confident than ever that I won't fuck this up too badly.

Using one of Easton's pillows, I prop his hips up just enough that I'll have easy access and then I squirt a generous amount of lube onto my fingers.

"Mmm," he purrs, reaching down to stroke himself as he watches me. "I'm liking where this is going so far."

"Good, but I hope you're not in any hurry because I've been dying to take my time with you," I warn.

"I've got all the time in the world."

I give him a wicked grin, ready to push the boundaries of his patience and learn how to make him beg for it. I watch his face as I slide my slicked fingers into the crease of his ass.

"River," he gasps, his voice desperate and strained as I delicately trace the tip of my finger around the rough pucker of his hole.

I've been imagining this so long, my entire life it feels like, even if I only met Easton a few months ago. Everything inside me is craving and aching for him, but I want to savor it. I circle his entrance again with the tip of my finger, applying the barest hint of pressure and shivering with pleasure at the way his hole gives way, letting me push in just a fraction. His inner muscles clench around me, and even though I have less than half an inch of my finger inside him, I can feel how tight and hot he is.

"More," Easton begs, his voice raw and ragged, his chest heaving, and his legs falling open wider, welcoming me in. The blush spreading up this throat and over his face is the most beautiful shade of pink I've ever seen. I wonder if I could capture it in a drawing. Maybe if I had enough time to memorize the exact shade.

I wrap my free hand around his ankle, bringing it up to rest on my shoulder. I turn my head and press a kiss to the swell of his calf, his coarse, dark hair tickling my lips as I do. His skin feels warm against mine, and his entire body trembles as I push my finger in deeper, slowly enough to memorize the exact feeling of his channel opening for me, the tug of his rim around my knuckle, the blazing heat of him.

Easton's hands twist in the bedsheets, his

knuckles turning white with how hard he's clenching them, his head thrown back against the pillow, his swollen lips parted on a low, breathy moan, and his dark brown nipples pebbled just like all of the goosebumps covering his skin, tears already forming at the corner of his eyes. I know he was embarrassed the first time he explained that he always cries when he orgasms, but there's something so moving about it. It's like he's so overwhelmed by the way it feels, the emotions need somewhere to go.

"I've never seen anything more beautiful in my life," I murmur, pressing my lips to his calf again, trailing them up to his knee as I continue to work my finger slowly inside him, feeling the clench and flutter of his channel around me.

"*Please*," he whines, bucking his hips up in obvious frustration, his cock bobbing in the air, dripping a string of clear, glistening precum onto his stomach, just below his belly button.

Such a pretty cock too. I may have never been with a man before, but I certainly spent a lot of time, especially in my teen years, thinking about cocks, drawing cocks, getting off on cock filled porn. And Easton has an absolutely perfect cock. It's not an intimidating monster cock that would've frankly scared me a little, but it's definitely not small either. It's thick enough to wrap my hand around and just make my fingers touch, the flared head a dark shade of pink from his arousal, with a slight curve toward his belly that

I bet at the right angle would hit my prostate just right.

My finger is as deep as I can push it, my last knuckle buried against his rim, and he clenches around me again, making a desperate noise in the back of his throat and jerking his hips again.

"*River*," he groans my name.

"So impatient," I tease, pulling my finger out an inch and then pushing it back in a little more roughly, making him gasp and clutch the sheets even harder in his fist. I crook my finger, finding the spongy spot inside him that makes his cock flex and his blush deepen.

I lick my lips and watch another drip of precum slick his stomach, the veins of his shaft begging to be memorized by my tongue. I dart my gaze up to his face again, and my breath catches at the almost painful pleasure painted there as I press against his prostate with the pad of my finger.

I lean forward, his leg that was hitched on my shoulder now laying across my back as I drag my tongue along his shaft from base to tip, the salty flavor of his skin and desire bursting on my tongue and making my mouth water. I flick my tongue along the little V where his head meets the shaft, and Easton lets out a little whine, squirming and thrusting toward my mouth impatiently.

While I tease him with my tongue, I pull my finger almost all the way out, and add a second one before I ease back in as slowly as I did before. I drag my tongue around the head of his cock, dipping the tip into his slit in search of more of his salty, tangy flavor and more ways to make him moan so deeply I swear his whole body shakes with it.

I wrap my lips around the head of his cock, and Easton lets out a strangled cry, his fingers finally untangling from the sheets to burrow into my hair.

"Oh fuck, oh fuck, oh fuck," he chants, his hips twitching and his body trembling as I crook my fingers to hit his prostate again, taking his cock deeper into my mouth.

It's a strange feeling to have my lips stretched around another man's cock, feel the weight of it against my tongue, the taste of his arousal dripping down my throat as I gently suck, using my tongue at the same time to trace the ridges and veins, learn the topography of him. I look up at his face again and see tears clinging to his long, dark eyelashes.

"So good," he gasps, and I can feel his cock thicken against my tongue as I guide my fingers over his prostate again.

My own cock is hard and aching and getting more uncomfortable with every addicting sound falling from Easton's lips.

I take his cock deeper into my throat, feeling an insatiable hunger to be filled by him, to make him feel pleasure like he's never felt before, to taste his cum and have it dripping from my lips. The head of his cock hits the back of my throat, and I gag, but strangely enough, that only makes me harder, makes me want to suck him deeper. I hump against the bed, grinding my cock against it.

Easton's hips buck, pushing himself down onto my fingers harder and then back up into my mouth with each thrust. He's careful not to push too deep into my throat, but I want to choke on him again, I want to take him too deep and wonder how I'll manage to breathe. I want to feel my throat constricting around his length.

I fuck my fingers into him harder, and I'm rewarded with gasps and groans and another rush of precum against my tongue. I push myself onto his cock deeper again, gagging for a second time and feeling my balls constrict and the sheets beneath me grow damp with precum as I shamelessly rut against the bed.

The third time I try to take Easton's cock deeper into my throat, I swallow at the same time his head hits the back of my throat, and I manage to take him all the way in. I groan with a deep satisfaction, and I can feel the sound vibrating through his shaft. His balls feel high and tight as they slap against my chin with each thrust of his cock into my mouth. I suck harder, teasing his prostate again with my fingers until I can feel the muscles in his thighs tensing, his grip in my hair tightening, his cock swelling between my lips.

"Oh god, River, I'm going to...I can't...oh god," he cries in warning.

I moan from deep in my chest as the first

burst of his release hits my tongue, saltier and thicker than the precum that came before it. His cock pulses between my lips; I can feel each pump of his seed before it even hits my tongue, and my own cock throbs in response. I continue to fuck against the bed as I swallow down every drop Easton gives me until my release washes over me, soaking the sheets as wave after wave of pleasure hits me.

When I finally let Easton's softening cock fall from between my lips, we're both breathless and trembling from aftershocks.

"You were lying when you said you hadn't done that before, right?" he jokes as I crawl up the bed to lay down next to him.

"No, was it good?"

Easton laughs. "That was incredible. Fuck, I think that actually killed a few brain cells."

I may be a dick sucking prodigy, but I still managed to jizz all over myself like a teenager, so I won't get too cocky about it.

We cuddle for a few minutes before I slip out of bed to clean myself up as best as I can, wash my hands, and rinse out my mouth. Not that I don't love the taste of Easton's cum on my lips, but I probably should've been more careful. We haven't even talked about STIs and with my suppressed immune system that could be seriously bad news. I push down my anxiety about it and take a deep breath before rinsing my mouth out with mouth-wash I find sitting on the bathroom counter. When

I return to the bedroom, Easton gives me a shy smile.

"I was thinking," he starts, stopping to clear his throat, dipping his head to avoid my eyes.

"Yes?" I ask with amusement, the panic that started setting in while I was in the bathroom easing a bit at the sight of Easton's smile. I just had my finger in his ass and his cock in my mouth; I'm not sure what he could be embarrassed to ask now.

"Would you, um...will you spend the night?"

My stomach does a little flip, and warmth spreads through my chest. I try not to sound too eager as I agree crawling into bed beside him.

It takes a minute for us to get situated and comfortable—all pillows properly fluffed and limbs arranged correctly. Easton rests his head against my chest, and I put an arm around him, our legs tangling as we cuddle close. His warm breath puffs against my chest, and a deep contentment blankets me. The loneliness I became so familiar with after my surgery has been ebbing since I met Easton, but the last tendrils of it slip away into the night, leaving me feeling lighter. My throat aches with words I know are premature, words that would no doubt scare Easton away. So, I hold him close and think the words as hard as I can, hoping some part of his heart will hear them whispered from mine.

"Listen, I don't want to ruin the moment or anything, but..." I clear my throat, heat creeping into my cheeks. *I'm an adult, having a conversation about safe sex isn't anything to feel uncomfortable with,* I scold myself.

"What is it?" Easton asks, trying to pull back so he can look at me. I tighten my grip on him, not wanting him to go anywhere.

"Nothing bad," I assure him. "I probably should've brought this up before actually, but because of the anti-rejection meds I have to take I have to be cautious with my immune system." I can feel him stiffening against me.

"Is it that bad? I know you have to wash your hands a lot, but should I be more cautious too?"

"It's not so bad," I assure him. "The first six months I had to be *really* cautious, but now my restrictions are things I'm pretty used to living with."

"Like with the gardening."

"Like with the gardening," I agree. "And with sex," I add.

"That makes sense." He turns his head a fraction and brushes a kiss to my chest. "I haven't been with anyone since Paul; I promise I don't have anything. But we can go to a free clinic this week to make sure."

"That would be great," I say, relief easing the knot in my chest.

"Your health is extremely important to me, River. If there's ever anything you need me to do to make sure you're safe, just tell me."

"I promise." I kiss the top of his head, and we both relax.

I run my fingers slowly through his hair as his breathing slows, and his body relaxes against mine. Sleep tugs at me too, but the moment feels too precious to risk missing. I hold him in the dark, memorizing the sound of his soft snores until I can't hold off falling asleep any longer, and I drift off with him.

CHAPTER 19

Easton

Waking up with a pair of arms around me, a body curved around mine from behind, soft, hot breath on the back of my neck, is so good it nearly brings tears to my eyes. I never thought I'd experience this again, and I didn't realize just how much I missed it.

I wiggle in his arms until he loosens his grip enough that I can roll over. I can still feel the stickiness from the lube in the crack of my ass, a little bit of soreness in my hole from being played with like it hasn't been in ages. Until River came along, I could hardly manage a half-hearted jerk session, let alone solo ass play.

River makes a contented humming sound in the back of his throat as I nuzzle my face into the crook of his neck. Everything feels warm and happy and content; all I want to do is keep sleeping for a while, just like this. So I do.

I drift in and out of sleep for a few more hours. When we happen to wake up at the same time, we trade soft, half-asleep kisses and unhurried touches before drifting back off. I'm pressed so tightly against him, I can feel his heartbeat against my chest, a rhythm I memorized in another lifetime. It's Paul's heartbeat, but it's River's too.

"You know what color I think this is?" River asks in a sleep-rough voice as I trail kisses along his shoulder.

"Mmm." I think for a moment, closing my eyes and *feeling* the moment, letting it wrap itself around me and burrow inside me. "It's azure," I decide. "Rich and beautiful and peaceful."

"I like that," he agrees before we drift into more peaceful sleep.

When we wake up for real sometime in the late morning, we still don't bother to drag ourselves out of bed right away. I rest my head on his chest, and we talk about nothing and everything.

I trail my fingers along the scar in the center of River's chest, feeling the steady rise and fall of his breaths, his skin warm against mine as we lay tangled. I try to imagine a more perfect place I could be in the world and nothing comes to mind.

"What happened?" I ask the question I've wondered about for years. "Why'd you need a new heart?"

"Bad luck mostly," he says. "It was a totally freak thing. I swear, when I was laying in that hospital bed for weeks, waiting to find out if I'd live or die, I started to believe in fate for the first time and I was sure my number was up."

"Were you in an accident?"

"No, I had strep throat," River gives a dry

sort of laugh. "One day I was bitching to Brandon about how bad my throat hurt and downing cough drops, and the next I was in the hospital because I couldn't catch my breath."

"Strep throat?" I repeat in disbelief. "How does strep throat make you need a heart transplant?"

"Like I said, bad luck, mostly. I guess when I was really young, I had hand, foot, and mouth virus, and no one knew it at the time, but the virus weakened my heart muscles. It can happen on occasion, the doctor said, and usually you'll be fine the rest of your life after that. Unfortunately for me, the strep bacteria attacked those already weakened muscles too."

"That's crazy."

"Yeah, when the doctor told me I'd need a heart transplant, or I'd be dead within a few weeks..." He shakes his head and tightens his grip on me. "Do you know the odds of getting a transplant at all let alone that quickly?"

"No," I breathe the word, feeling my stomach constrict and my chest flutter.

"They suck," River explains succinctly. "You know, I always used to say if I knew I was dying, I'd make the most of my last weeks or months, go on a tropical vacation or go skydiving or something. But all I could do was lay there in that fucking bed with the smell of antiseptic making me sick and the drone of shitty daytime TV driving me insane and wait to die."

My eyes burn with unshed tears. I tilt my head and press a kiss to River's jaw. His eyes are glassy and haunted in a way I haven't seen them before.

"That must've been awful."

"You know what I thought about the most?" he asks.

"What?"

"I thought about how I'd never loved someone. I felt like it was a blessing and a curse because I'd never known what it was like to be so crazy over someone, I'd do anything for them, *be* anything for them. But I was glad there wasn't anyone there who had to cry over my bed and wonder with me if I'd live to see my next birthday." River chokes out a sob and uses his freehand to wipe his face. "Sorry, that's fucking depressing. It all worked out in the end, right?"

"Right," I murmur, a surreal feeling settling over me. He talked about fate, and before Paul I always rolled my eyes at things like that. There's no fate, only things that happen that we try to make sense of. But maybe things worked out exactly how they were planned.

The thought nearly chokes me as I press my face into the side of River's throat and hold him close. A wracking cry rolls through me, my tears spilling over his skin, wrapping both arms around me. His tears wet my hair as he puts a cheek against the top of my head, and our bodies tremble together as we both cry. Tears of mourning, tears of acceptance, tears of happiness that we somehow managed to be here together in this moment in spite of everything—they're all there, baptizing our souls and making us new again.

When the tears eventually slow, my lips find River's. The kiss is slow and impossibly sweet, our lips moving against each other without a hurry. My hands burn a roadmap over his skin of all the places I've been before and can't wait to go again. His arms are so tight around me that I have no doubt he needs an anchor in this moment just as much as I do.

"Do you think someone can have more than one soulmate?" I ask against his lips. "Or is that being too greedy?"

"I honestly don't know," he confesses, trailing hot kisses down the column of my throat. "All I know is that being with you feels more right than anything else ever has."

River

I didn't know I was still so affected by my near-death experience so many years ago, but it feels good to hold Easton and cry—it feels healing. Eventually we get ourselves together and get out of bed.

"I can't stay too long today," I let him know as we get dressed, putting back on the pajama pants I borrowed from him last night after our shower. "Since I didn't plan on staying over, I don't have my meds with me, and I need to take them every morning."

"Oh, of course. Can you stay for breakfast, or do you have to go right away?"

I wrap my arms around Easton and nibble his neck. "Breakfast sounds good."

"I'm not on the menu this morning," he teases.

"Too bad."

On our way to the kitchen, we pass through the living room and my eyes land on Easton's work desk, panels for his next graphic novel laid out.

"Oh my god, is this a sequel to *Hotel Nowhere*?" I gasp, picking up one of the papers, my eyes roaming over it greedily.

"No spoilers," he scolds, pinching my ass again and snatching the paper from my hand when I yelp.

"Come on, just a few pages?" I beg, pushing out my bottom lip in an exaggerated pout as my inner fanboy loses his mind. "I'll blow you again."

He snorts a laugh. "Wow, is that all this relationship is to you? You're just using me to get to my work," he feigns offense.

"It's more of a bonus," I reason, looping my arms around his waist and pressing my nose into his messy head of curls.

"Nice try, but you're not reading it early."

"You're mean," I complain with a laugh.

In the kitchen, I start the electric tea kettle while Easton pulls out a carton of eggs from the refrigerator. I take a seat at the counter and watch him get breakfast ready, a smile on his lips as he moves about the kitchen. When he turns toward the sink, his gaze snags on the window, and he stills. There's a far away look in his eyes for several seconds before his smile returns.

"The garden looks beautiful," he says. "I forgot how nice it is to look out the back window and see it bursting with color."

I get up and move to stand behind him to look out the window as well.

"It does look great. You did a fantastic job."

"*We* did," he corrects.

"I didn't do much but dig holes for you."

"I wouldn't have even pulled out the weeds if it wasn't for you. You made me *want* to put the color back into my life."

I kiss him again because I can't get enough of his lips and because I love the way he always smiles afterward.

CHAPTER 20

Easton

"You know what I want?" I muse out loud with my head resting on River's chest, the beating of his heart whooshing like the ocean in my ear. It's been two weeks since River spent the night at my house and having him in my bed seems to have become an addiction.

"Tell me and I'll make it happen," he promises, and my heart flutters.

"Why?" I ask with amusement. "Shouldn't you make me work a little harder for it or something?"

"I don't know. I just know that making you smile feels as vital as breathing. I don't understand it either; I just know it feels right."

The amusement bleeds out of me, replaced by complete awe and the ever-present guilt about the fact that I'm lying to him.

It's on the tip of my tongue to tell him I love him, that I didn't think I'd ever love anyone but Paul until he came along to turn my world upside down and reminded me how it feels to smile. But it feels so unfair to say it until I find a way to tell him the truth.

"I want to go to the beach," I finally finish my initial thought. "Have you ever been to North Carolina?"

"No," he says. "Let's go."

"Yeah?" I can feel myself lighting up at the idea. "When?"

"I have vacation time. Let's go now."

"Now?" I repeat with a laugh. "It's six o'clock on a Sunday night."

"Sure, why not? I'll send my boss an email and tell him I'm taking vacation this week, and we can make a road trip out of it. It can't be that far."

"Seriously? We're going to do this?"

"Hell yes, we're going to do this," River says, rolling me onto my back and crawling on top of me to kiss me breathless. "Start packing while I send an email, and then we can jump on Airbnb and see if there's anywhere to rent last minute."

"I can't believe we're really doing this." I feel a little giddy as River climbs off me, and I scramble off the bed, grabbing my suitcase from the closet and starting to chuck clothes into it. "This is crazy."

"A little bit of crazy every now and again is good for the soul," he advises wisely, getting off the bed and wrapping his arms around me. "I'm going to run home and pack, and I'll be back soon, okay?"

"Okay," I agree with a smile, giving him one last kiss before he leaves.

I pack my clothes and an unopened bottle

of lube I just picked up yesterday, and then head to the bathroom to get my toiletries. On my way, I stop and head to the living room, grabbing my colored pencils and sketchbook on impulse and taking them back to the bedroom to put into my suitcase.

We got our test results back last week. Unsurprisingly, we were both negative, but I still breathed a sigh of relief when I got them. I didn't have any reason to think otherwise, but I worried anyway. The thought that getting caught up in the moment like we did, when he went down on me bare, could've been so dangerous for River was more than I could take. I had nightmares all week about River getting sick, having to be hospitalized, dying. My heart jumps into my throat as I recall the dreams, my palms growing sweaty. I've already lived the horror of losing someone; I don't think I can take that again.

River returns an hour later with a packed suitcase and his laptop bag. We settle back onto the bed and search for a rental property for the week, agreeing to splurge a little and treat ourselves to a place right on the beach. It's not like we can't afford it between the two of us, but it certainly feels extravagant. Hell, it has to be more than I've spent on myself in the past five years combined, but that's because I was existing instead of living for so long.

"You know what color this is?" I ask, cuddling into his side once we've booked our rental and planned our driving route for the morning.

"What color is it?"

"Daisy yellow," I say. "Bright and happy and exciting."

"That's a good color." River brushes a kiss to the top of my head. "We should get some sleep; we have a long drive ahead of us tomorrow."

"Sleep sounds good, but there's one thing I have to do first," I tease, slipping under the covers to show him just how much I appreciate this impromptu vacation plan.

River

It's still dark out when my alarm goes off the next morning. Easton grumbles in his sleep and clings to me harder when I try to wiggle out of his grasp to get out of bed. I huff out a half-asleep laugh and kiss his cheek, prying his fingers from my shirt and managing to slip away.

I use the bathroom and take my medication using water from the sink to wash it down, and then I hop in the shower. When I get out, Easton is still fast asleep, and I smile to myself as I watch him. It's easy to imagine a daily routine where I get up early for work and he sleeps in. He'd have a lunch already packed for me, waiting in the refrigerator, with a sweet note inside. I could leave him notes too, sitting on the counter for him to find when he gets up. I think I'd like that—scratch that, I *know* I'd like it. The thought of a life shared with him makes my chest ache with longing and my throat constrict. Sure, there have been women in the past I've considered a long-term future with, but it's never felt like *this*. It's never felt so necessary to be with someone the way it does with Easton.

Easton's words from a couple weeks ago come back to my mind—*is it possible to have two soulmates.* I'm not sure I ever believed in soulmates, but the minute I heard the word on his lips, it felt right, like everything else with Easton has. And the fact that he's thinking those things makes me believe he feels it too.

"Are you watching me sleep like a creep?" he asks with sleepy amusement, his eyes still closed, but the dimple on his cheek just starting to appear as he tries to hide his smile.

"Just trying to decide on an interesting way to wake you."

"Mmmm, I have a few ideas. Come back to bed, and I'll show you," he tempts, holding up the covers to beckon me. I groan, readily imagining how warm and cozy it would feel to climb back in next to him, how his body would mold to mine, his erection tenting his thin boxers and pushing up against me. I can practically feel his hot mouth scorching a path over my skin as he wraps his hand around me and pumps slowly. My cock jerks in response, thickening beneath the towel.

"If I let you lure me back into bed, we're going to blow our whole schedule for the day," I point out with absolutely no conviction.

"I'm sorry, all I heard was blow," Easton teases, giving me a wicked smile.

What the hell, it won't kill us to be an hour behind schedule.

I drop my towel and crawl back into bed. Wrapping my hands around Easton's waist, I tug him on top of me. His lips find mine instantly, and that's all it takes to get lost in him for a while.

*****

"We're late," Easton laments as we load our suitcases into the car, well past nine a.m., *three* hours past the time we planned to leave.

"Totally worth it," I assure him with a wink.

"Absolutely," he agrees. "You know, we should've flown. An eight-hour drive seemed a lot shorter yesterday than it does this morning."

A twinge of guilt makes me grimace. "Sorry."

"Why are you sorry? Are you afraid of flying or something?"

"Yeah, but not for the reason you think," I say as we both climb into the car and pull out of the driveway.

"What do you mean?"

"I'm not afraid of a plane crash; I know that's rare," I explain. "I'm afraid of getting sick."

"Oh," Easton says, and I can practically hear the wheels turning as he processes it. "The recycled air, you're breathing everyone's germs. So, you can't fly *at all*?"

"I could probably wear an anti-viral mask over my mouth and nose," I reason. "But I guess if it's not *necessary* I'd rather not take the risk."

"That makes total sense. I would never want you to take an unnecessary risk," he agrees, reaching over and putting a hand over mine. "I never thought about all the ways we're exposed to diseases. It's so easy to take a healthy immune system for granted."

"I totally get it. Before I got sick, I probably would've eaten a hot dog off a gas station floor," I joke, and Easton makes a gagging sound. "The first six months were especially hard because you're at an even higher risk while you're healing, and the doctors are making sure the dosages of anti-rejection meds are right, but it's really not so bad now. I have to be more conscious than other people, but I'm used to it," I say apologetically. Will this be too much for Easton to want to deal with long-term? Always having to consider things that might put me at risk.

"As long as you're safe and healthy, I don't mind at all," he assures me, leaning over the center console to kiss my cheek before settling back into his seat.

The drive ends up taking ten hours once we factor in stops to stretch our legs and eat, and it's just after seven when we pull into the driveway of the beach house.

It's a cute little one-story bungalow with a deck off the back that leads right onto the beach.

We drop our bags in the bedroom and decide a walk is in order before the tide gets too high.

Easton links his hand through mine, and I'm not sure I can think of anything more cliché or perfect than walking hand in hand on the beach. Our feet sink into the soft sand, and the waves lap at our ankles.

"I'm already glad we did this," Easton says with a happy sigh. "I didn't realize until just now, but I haven't been away from that house in over five years. I mean, I go out to buy groceries or spend time with Fox, but aside from that…" he trails off and shakes his head. "I can't believe how much of life I've been missing out on until you came along."

"You needed time to grieve; there's nothing wrong with that," I point out.

"I did," he agrees. "But I'm really glad you came along and saved me from myself when you did."

"Me too." I say. Stopping to face him, I cup his face in one hand and tilt it so I can press my lips to his in a soft kiss.

We walk a little farther down the beach, talking about things we'd like to do while we're here and eventually turn to walk back to the house. Since the last thing either of us wants to do is run to the store for groceries after spending all day in the car, we order dinner and eat it on the back porch, enjoying the sound of the crashing ocean and the colors of the sky as it turns to night.

"Tell me a secret no one else knows," I prompt playfully, leaning back in the chaise lounge chair to watch the stars as they emerge.

"A secret *no one* knows?" Easton repeats skeptically.

"It's fine if Paul knew," I amend.

"Hmm, I still have to think about that. I'm not a big secret keeper," he says. "I've never been very good at it." Something guilty flashes across his face for so brief a second, I wonder if I imagined it.

"Okay, just tell me something I don't know about you yet," I concede.

"I'm terrified of jellyfish," he confesses solemnly. "I can handle spiders and snakes and whatever else, but jellyfish are terrifying."

"Well, good news, I already looked it up, and the jellyfish they have here don't sting, so it's safe if you see any on the beach."

"I'll still keep a wide berth, thanks." He shudders. "Your turn, tell me a secret or something I don't know."

"When I was in high school, I'd hide under the bleachers to watch the football players and cheerleaders practice. It was like a bisexual wet dream," I admit with a smirk, and Easton laughs.

"I can totally see that. I bet there was at least one football player who would've been into you if he'd known it was an option."

I blush and wave him off. "No way."

"Come on, have you seen you?" Easton insists. "You're insanely sexy."

"You're biased."

"Mmm, fair enough. I'm fine with that because I don't like to share anyway."

"No sharing," I agree, leaning over to kiss the side of his neck, feeling his pulse jump against my lips. "What do you say we take this to the bedroom?"

He raises an eyebrow at me. "I like that plan."

CHAPTER 21

Easton

We tumble together onto the bed, hands groping wildly, our bodies moving against each other in a rhythm we've learned over the past couple of months. I've been all for taking this slow, but it seems like River is ready to take his foot off the brakes, and I'm *all* for that too.

It would probably be easier to undress if we stopped groping and kissing, but neither of us seems willing to make that sacrifice, so we fumble through undressing while our tongues tangle and our hands slow us down in all the best ways.

I moan against River's lips as he reaches into my boxers and wraps his hand around my aching arousal, giving me a few slow, teasing strokes.

"I want to make love to you," River says in a deep, throaty voice as he kisses along my jaw and down the column of my throat.

I'm torn between teasing him for the cheesy wording and chiding him that everything we do is making love, but the ability to form words eludes me as he cups my balls in his hand, his index finger slipping into the crease of my ass, so close to my hole.

"Please," I gasp, tilting my hips to encourage him to give me more.

River's laugh rumbles from his chest to mine, making me ache all the more to feel him naked against me, around me, inside of me.

I manage to pry my hands off of him long enough to shove my underwear down and kick them out of the way and then do the same for River's, finally getting us both completely naked. His body against mine is delicious heat and friction, lighting me up inside and feeding the addiction that's grown with each hit of River I've gotten.

His dry finger brushes over my hole again, and I let my legs fall open wide in invitation.

"Hold on, baby, let me get the lube."

I whine in protest as he climbs off the bed and rummages through his suitcase for a minute, holding up a fresh bottle of lube victoriously.

Fingering me has become one of River's favorite past times in the last two weeks, and there's a lot to be said for the whole *practice makes perfect* thing, because damn, does the man know his way around my ass.

My breath hitches as he circles my hole with his now slicked finger, teasing the rim as his tongue flicks against my nipples, alternating one and then the other. My cock stands painfully hard, the tip glistening with precum. When he finally slips his finger inside me, I nearly sob with relief.

"More," I beg in a shaky, rough voice that

makes River rumble in approval, his tongue vibrating against my nipple as he licks it.

I writhe and beg, but River takes his sweet time playing with my hole, making sure I'm pliant and slick and open for him before he *finally* reaches for the lube again to coat his cock. The upside of needing the STD tests done already was we had the chance to talk about going bare.

River shifts around so he's sitting with his back against the headboard of the bed, and then crooks a finger at me. I raise an interested eyebrow and climb into his lap.

"I want it just like this so I can kiss you, is that okay?" he asks, grabbing my ass cheeks with both hands, his eyes boring into mine with an intensity that takes my breath away.

"Works for me," I agree, wiggling into position and then reaching down to hold his cock straight and steady, slowly lowering myself onto him.

The burn as his head breaches my first ring of tight muscles reminds me exactly how long it's been since I've had anything bigger than a few fingers up there. River's hands on my hips steady me, his lips finding mine as I adjust to the feeling of being so full before I ease farther down, taking him in deeper and filling myself up.

His tongue slides against mine hot and wet, my arms wrapped around his neck as I ease inch by inch onto his cock. When he's finally buried to the hilt, I test the feeling by swiveling my hips, drawing a moan from both of us.

"God, you feel incredible," River murmurs against my lips, his hands on my hips encouraging me to move, not that I need encouragement.

I pant and moan, my breath puffing out against River's collarbone, our sweat slicked bodies rocking together, his cock so deep inside me it's hard to tell where he ends and I begin. His thrusts are slow and rhythmic, keeping me right on the edge of sanity, my erection dragging against his stomach with each movement, his hands gentle on my hips, his lips trailing over my skin with the occasional flick of his tongue.

My balls ache as his length presses against my prostate each time he rocks his hips forward, my precum mixing with the sweat on his stomach to make a hot, wet surface with just the right amount of friction.

"You feel so good," he murmurs against my flesh, his warm breath making goosebumps rise under his lips. "God, Easton, I..." he gasps, his grip tightening. I moan in agreement with whatever he was going to say.

I drag my hands through his damp hair, down his broad shoulders, over his biceps. I want to touch every inch of him, I want to imprint every detail of this moment onto my soul.

I want to shove him flat onto the bed and ride him faster, harder, to chase the orgasm building slowly inside me like liquid fire, but I can't bring myself to do anything but whimper and feel every one of his maddeningly slow thrusts.

"River," I gasp his name, loving the shape of it on my tongue while he fills me beyond comprehension. The aching need inside me brings tears to my eyes, spilling over onto my cheeks as I clench around his length to feel him all the more intensely.

"Oh fuck, Easton," he groans, wrapping his arms fully around my waist to pull me even more tightly against him. I tilt my head down, and his lips are on my cheeks, kissing away each tear as it falls. The building feeling in the pit of my stomach becomes more intense, precum leaking freely from me like a leaky faucet, every pulse of my heartbeat thundering in my cock as it throbs between us.

I clench around him again, my breath hitching as I feel the first flutter of my orgasm just barely out of reach. River gasps, and it almost sounds like a sob as it shudders through his entire body, making him tremble against me.

His next thrust makes me see stars, my balls constricting, heat clawing at my skin as my muscles all tense, ready to snap at any second. Deep inside me, I can feel his cock swell, his breath coming in shallow pants as he rocks faster, more desperately.

"Easton," he moans my name again. "Easton," he groans.

"Yes. Yes. Yes," I chant, digging my fingers into his flesh as my eyes roll back in my head, the building tension finally giving way as he pegs my prostate one last time, pushing me over the edge. My cock pulses against his stomach, thick spurts of cum trickling over his skin as my ass clenches and releases around him.

River lets out a strangled cry, his forehead pressed against mine, the throbbing release of his own orgasm echoing mine. "I love you," he gasps.

His words wrap themselves around me and leave me aching with a chaotic mess of emotions—guilt, joy, confusion, desperation. It clogs my throat and keeps me from doing anything but closing my eyes and focusing on the feeling of our still joined bodies until his softening cock slips out of me, and he lays back, taking me with him.

River doesn't say anything else. He runs his hands slowly through my hair, over my back, over my leg that's still hitched over his waist now that we're laying down. He makes content little humming noises in the back of his throat, but he doesn't say another word. I lay still with my eyes closed until his hands stop moving, and his breathing slows, then I slip out of bed as quietly as possible, grabbing my phone and taking it to the bathroom.

I'm trembling as I ease myself down onto the cold, tile floor. The sweat cooling on my skin has me shivering, my sticky cum turning crusty on my stomach. But all I can do is sit there and replay River's words of love over and over again, my chest constricting more each time. When my hands stop trembling enough that I can actually dial my phone, I make a call.

"Hello?" Fox asks in a gruff, half-asleep voice.

I open my mouth to say hi back, but a sob escapes instead.

"East? What's the matter? Are you okay?" he asks in a rush, clearly wide awake now. "Do you need me to come over?"

"I'm not at home," I manage to say as tears flow down my cheeks, and I drag in short breaths.

"Where are you? I'll come get you."

"In North Carolina," I say with a laugh that turns into another sob.

"What's going on? You're scaring me."

"River told me he loves me."

Fox lets out a sigh, and I hear rustling like he's lying back down in bed now that he knows I'm not in grave danger. "What's the problem? You don't love him?"

"I do. But what if..."

"What if you only love him because of Paul?"

"No," I say, pulling my legs up to my chest and pressing the phone harder to my ear as my worst fear bubbles past my lips. "What if *he* only loves *me* because of Paul?"

"What?" he asks. "What are you talking about? He doesn't even know about the heart, does he?"

"No, but..." I take a deep breath, now that

the tears have stopped, and try to gather my thoughts to explain. "I watched this thing once where this guy got a kidney transplant and all of a sudden he had new favorite foods and stuff. What if River only loves me because Paul loved me?"

"I don't know," Fox admits. "I don't think there's any way of knowing that, but the way he looks at you..." He trails off for a second before continuing. "I think it's real. I think that man loves you just as much as Paul did for all his own reasons."

"You think?" I ask, hope pushing the other emotions out of my chest for the first time.

"I really do. This situation is fucked up, we both know that, but we only have this one life, and I think we owe it to ourselves to find every bit of happiness we can. After Paul, I didn't think you'd ever be happy again, but River changed that."

"Are you mad I'm with someone else?"

"Not mad, but it *is* a little weird to see you all in love with someone else. It sort of throws my world off center to see the looks you used to give Paul now directed at someone else. But it's good, East, it's really good. You deserve to be happy; it's what he would've wanted."

"I know," I agree, not feeling annoyed by those words for the first time. "Thank you."

"Any time, you know that," he says. "But, East, you've gotta tell him. If you love him and this is for real, he has to know."

"What if he hates me when he finds out?"

"He still deserves to know," he says firmly.

"Yeah, I'll tell him," I promise.

"Good. Now, go back to your man and let me get some sleep."

I chuckle, wiping my cheeks and using the edge of the sink to pull myself to a standing position.

"Okay. Love you, Fox."

"Love you too, East."

River

I wake up to find myself alone in bed. I reach for Easton's side and find it cool to the touch. Sitting up, I rub my hands over my eyes and look around. The clock says it's just after five in the morning. The first remnants of morning light are peeking through the windows. I notice the curtains by the sliding door fluttering, so I slip out of bed to see if Easton is out there.

I stop when I spot him, sitting in the lounge chair with a sketchbook in his lap, his hand moving furiously over it as he glances back and forth between it and the pink, orange sunrise lighting up the sky. I look a little closer and realize he's using his colored pencils to draw it, and my heart feels full to bursting.

I slide open the door as quietly as possible and step out onto the porch. Easton barely glances in my direction, but the smile on his lips tells me he knows I'm here. I slip into the chair beside him and lean back to watch the sun come up with him.

It feels like more than just the start of a new day, it feels like the first day of the rest of our lives.

"River," he says quietly, the sound of his colored pencil scratching against the paper stopping. "I love you too."

The words send my heart into a gallop, a smile spreading across my lips in an instant.

I know it wasn't fair of me to say it while I was inside of him last night; I hadn't even meant to. I'd just been so overwhelmed with the moment it slipped out. I certainly wasn't expecting him to say it back anytime soon.

"Can I..." He looks over at me with a shy smile.

"Anything," I tell him honestly. If he asked me for the moon, the sun, the entire galaxy I'd find a way to give it to him, just to see him smile.

"Would you mind if I came to sit in your lap?" he asks. "I don't want to crush you or anything."

"Get your ass over here." I pat my lap, and he sets his art supplies down, scrambling over to me without hesitation. Easton leans his head back against my shoulder, and we watch the sunrise in silence for a while, the feeling of him in my arms better than anything I can imagine, our steady breathing and the crashing of the ocean the only sound in the world.

CHAPTER 22

River

One week at the beach wasn't nearly enough. Not enough splashing in the ocean, not enough sitting on the back porch late into the night sharing secrets and stories from our lives, not enough chances to hear Easton whisper words of love as I moved inside his body, driving us both insane with pleasure.

"We should make this a yearly trip," I suggest as we barrel down the highway toward home. It's not until the words are out that I realize how they sound—like there's no doubt we'll still be together a year from now, two years, three. My heart beats faster, full of longing and hope. I want it all with Easton—a shared home, a future, every day of the rest of our lives.

"That would be nice," he says agreeably, reaching over the center console and lacing our fingers together. I breathe a sigh of relief that we seem to be on the same page.

The drive goes by quickly in a blur of snacks and road trip karaoke and laughter. When we pass a road sign for Browerton, Pennsylvania, a pang hits me in the chest.

"Hey, how would you feel about a short detour?" I ask.

"If there's a bathroom I'm all for it," Easton says.

"It's my Mom's place," I explain. "She lives close to here, and I haven't seen her in a while. I could introduce you to her, and, you know, get around to telling her I'm bi."

"Right now?" he asks with a hint of uncertainty. "I don't want you to feel like you need to do that for me. If you aren't ready to be out at work or to your mom or wherever, it's not a problem for me."

"It was never about not being ready. I guess I just didn't see any reason to tell her when I was dating women. I always figured that if I ever dated a guy seriously, I'd tell her. I wasn't hiding it. She just tends to be dramatic, so I was just avoiding the headache of it." I take the next exit toward her place, and I notice Easton chewing his bottom lip out of the corner of my eye.

"Is it too soon for the whole *meet the parent* thing?" I guess. "We don't have to do this; we can hold off."

"No...it's, um..." He squirms in his seat and then lets out a little sigh. "It's fine, we can do this. Why pass up the opportunity if we're this close, right?"

"Right," I parrot, a smile creeping over my lips.

"Do you and your mom get along?" he asks

as we turn into a neighborhood.

"We get along fine. Like I said, she can be a tad dramatic, so I probably don't call or visit as often as I should. It's horrible to say, but when I was in the hospital, I dreaded her visits. She would just stand over me and cry like she was at my funeral or something. It was horrible."

"I'm sorry. I'm sure it wasn't an easy situation for her."

"No, I know that."

Before long, we're pulling into the driveway of her little ranch house with the overgrown lawn. I shake my head at myself. She only lives two hours away; I could make the effort to come out here more, mow her lawn from time to time.

"You sure you're ready for this?" Easton checks, giving my hand a squeeze as I turn off the car.

"Ready as I'll ever be."

The front door swings open before we even reach the porch, my mom bursting out and hurrying over to pull me into a hug.

"I looked out the window, and I couldn't believe my eyes," she says as she squeezes me. "Is everything okay? I wasn't expecting you."

More guilt swamps me. "Everything's great. I was just in the area and thought I'd swing by."

"It's perfect timing; I was just putting tea on." She ushers us inside, so excited she doesn't even notice Easton until we all step into the house. "I'm so sorry, how rude of me. Are you a friend of River's?"

She extends a hand, and Easton reaches out to shake it with an uncertain smile on his face.

"I'm Easton," he says. "I'm…" He shoots me a glance, and I shrug. *No time like the present.*

"Mom, this is my boyfriend."

"I'm sorry?" She cocks her head, still absently holding Easton's hand, who's looking increasingly uncomfortable. I put my arm over his shoulders and give her my best boyish smile.

"Easton is my boyfriend. We've been seeing each other a few months, and it's pretty serious."

"Oh." She sounds dazed as she releases his hand and puts a smile back on her face, studying me for a few seconds. "Is it safe? With your heart, I mean."

I roll my eyes. "No less safe than sex with a woman," I assure her, and she blushes before looking back at Easton.

"He almost died," she says matter of factly. "He went into the hospital with strep throat and nearly died."

"I know," he says, his voice sounding thick. "I know how hard that must've been for you. My husband died six years ago, and the loss was unimaginable. I'm sure you were terrified of losing him. I bet you still are."

Her expression softens, and she pulls him into a hug. I hear sniffling, and I'm not sure which of them is crying, but this was definitely *not* how I expected their first meeting to go.

Easton

Crying on my boyfriend's mother's shoulder, not exactly what I was expecting when River decided we were going to stop by for a visit. But there's something oddly healing about the experience, feeling her slim body tremble as she cries right along with me. She nearly lost River, and I can tell it still haunts her. I bet she wakes up in the middle of the night in a cold sweat after nightmares of him dying.

"I just wish the hospital would've told us the name of the donor's family, so we could've thanked them properly," she says with a sniffle, finally pulling away, both of us using our hands to wipe away our tears.

A familiar guilt rolls through me. I need to tell the truth. River deserves to know. This isn't a fling; this isn't casual. He brought me to meet his mother. He told me he loves me. I have to tell him the truth.

"This is a bit heavy, no?" River says, putting an arm around me again. "Why don't we sit down, and you can get to know Easton a little, without any talk of dying."

"You're right," she agrees, smiling again and waving us down the hall toward the kitchen.

His mom makes tea and, just like River requested, the conversation turns lighter. I tell her about my job and my garden, she tells me stories about River as a child and even pulls out some photo albums to show me baby pictures. For the record, he was the cutest kid in the entire world.

But the guilt stays churning in my stomach. Every second, this lie weighs more heavily on me.

We visit for a few hours, and she tries to convince us to spend the night. River promises to come back more often, and she demands he brings me along, which makes me blush happily. My own parents weren't too thrilled when I came out, so it's nice to get a big motherly hug before we leave.

"River," she says as we slip our shoes back on by the front door. "Why didn't you tell me sooner? Did you think I wouldn't love you if I knew you were gay?"

"I'm not gay," he corrects her. "I like women too. I haven't dated a man before Easton, and I didn't see any reason to upset you unnecessarily."

"You being your true self is *never* unnecessary," she says firmly. "I don't care who you love; you're still my son."

He pulls her into a hug and then gives her a smacking kiss on the cheek. "I love you, Mom."

"I love you too."

We get back into the car, and I can see in River's eyes that he feels bad he hasn't been the most present son. I put a hand over his and give him a reassuring squeeze.

"It's never too late," I assure him.

He nods solemnly. "You're right. I'm going to make an effort from now on."

As we get back onto the highway, my heart

starts beating a little faster. I know I should tell him. I shouldn't put it off any longer, he deserves to know. I pull my hand off his and wipe my sweaty palm on my jeans.

"River, I—" The words lodge in my throat. How do I start this? How do I tell him I've been lying to him since we met? Maybe the car isn't the best place. What if he's so upset, he crashes? Or what if he wants to get away from me once I tell him? I shouldn't force him to be trapped with me for two more hours. It's waited this long, it can wait a little longer.

"Yeah?" he prompts when I don't finish my sentence.

"I love you," I say instead, and he smiles, reaching for my hand and lifting it to his lips.

"I love you too."

The last two hours of the trip are mostly silent. When we pull into my driveway, I consider just blurting out the truth, but he deserves better than that. I'll take a few days to plan how I'll tell him, and then I'll sit him down and be honest. My stomach clenches at the thought.

"I had a lot of fun this week," he says, looking over at me from his spot in the driver's seat. He didn't unbuckle, so I'm assuming he isn't planning to come in. I get it, we've been together all week, he probably needs to get home and make sure he collects his mail and has a little time to himself.

"Me too. It was amazing." I unbuckle and lean over to kiss him, his lips warm and pliant under mine, still tasting faintly of the sun and salt-water from the beach.

"I'll give you a call tomorrow. Sleep well."

"You too."

As soon as I step into my quiet house, I wish I'd tried to talk him into staying. In six years, I've gotten more than used to having an empty house all to myself, but River has spoiled me. He brought laughter and color back into my life, and now I don't think I can do without it again.

Bile rises in my throat at the thought of how he might react when I tell him the truth. He could leave; I wouldn't blame him if he did. He may hate me, and I wouldn't blame him for that either.

Just a little longer. I want to keep him a little longer before I tell him.

CHAPTER 23

River

I'm grinning from ear to ear as I stand on Easton's doorstep waiting for him to answer, bouncing a little with excitement.

When the door finally opens, I waste no time scooping my boyfriend up into my arms and kissing him soundly. He laughs against my lips, his arms instantly going around my neck as I lift him off the ground.

"Why hello," he says with a smile when I set him back on his feet.

"Get changed, we're going out to celebrate," I tell him, spinning him around and giving him a playful slap on the ass to get him moving. He turns his head to look at me over his shoulder, raising an eyebrow at me. "Please?" I add and that seems to mollify him.

I follow Easton into the house and down the hall to his bedroom, plopping down on his bed as he goes to his closet.

"What exactly are we celebrating? I need to know how to dress."

"Nothing major," I play it cool, fighting a smile. "Just my book getting picked up by a big, fancy, New York publisher."

"What?" Easton gasps, spinning around to face me with a huge grin. "Are you fucking kidding me?" He bounces onto the bed and crawls on top of me.

"I'm not kidding."

"Oh my god, this is huge!" he squeals, covering my face in kisses. I laugh and wrap my arms around his middle, pulling him closer and claiming his lips in an enthusiastic, unsophisticated kiss full of passion and excitement and lots of tongue.

"Do you want a celebratory blowjob before or after we go out to a fancy dinner?" he asks.

"After," I decide. "That anticipation is half the fun." He quirks his eyebrow at me again. "Well, maybe not *half*, but anticipation *is* fun."

"Fair enough. Let me get dressed, and we can go."

He kisses me once more before rolling off me and getting off the bed. He picks out an outfit and makes a show of undressing, swaying his hips to imaginary music as he slowly lowers his pants, shooting me a flirty smirk over his shoulder, his dimple on full display. My chest literally aches with how much I love him. It's too much and not enough all at once.

All his clothes make it to the hamper, and he stands stark naked near the foot of the bed, his back to me so I have the perfect view of his perky little ass. I sit up and scoot to the end of the bed, wrapping one arm around his waist and using my other hand to cup one of his sweet ass cheeks. My lips trail along the soft, warm skin on his back, along his shoulder blades and up the back of his neck. Easton lets out a soft moan, pressing his ass harder into my palm.

"You're the best thing that's ever happened to me," I murmur, and he stiffens in my arms. His breath catching and his body jolting before he tries to wriggle out of my grasp. "What? What's wrong?"

I let him go and see the pain written clearly on his face as he takes a big step away from me, tears shining in his eyes.

"What'd I do?" I ask, panic icing my veins.

"Sorry, it's not your fault," he assures me, his voice coming out choked. "That was...fuck." He clears his throat and takes a breath. "That was the last thing Paul ever said to me."

"I'm so sorry," I say, reaching my hand out to touch him and then thinking better of it and pulling back quickly. "I didn't know. I'm sorry."

"No, no." He turns to face me, taking my face between his hands and staring into my eyes. "It's a beautiful thing to say. I didn't mean to react like that."

"It was an understandable reaction," I tell him, carefully putting my hands on his hips.

"I don't know why you put up with me when I'm this fucked up. You were trying to be sweet, and I freaked out."

"Hey," I say, tightening my grip on his waist. "You are the most incredible person I've ever met. You lost someone you loved. I understand there are going to be difficulties that come with that. This isn't just some casual thing for me, Easton. I love you, and I'm *all in* with this. You can cry, freak out, whatever you need to do. *Nothing* is going to change my mind about this. I'm completely in love with you."

If anything, this seems to make him feel worse, a few more tears leaking from his eyes. He leans down and brushes a kiss to my mouth.

"I don't deserve you," he says.

"You deserve everything," I contradict him. "No more tears; this is a happy night, okay?"

"Okay," he agrees.

Easton

I can't believe I freaked out like that. I'm still embarrassed about it as River leads me into a nice Italian restaurant where he made us reservations. What are the odds that he'd use the exact words Paul used to say to me every day? It felt like some sort of sign, maybe a message from Paul somehow. But a message about what? Was it Paul's blessing for this relationship or a way of making me feel guilty for falling in love with someone else? Or maybe the ghost of my dead husband *didn't* speak through my current boyfriend— that's a possibility too, I suppose. I shake my head at myself. Maybe I should call my therapist again.

The hostess leads us to our table and offers us some wine. Which, to my surprise, River accepts.

"I thought you didn't drink?"

"One glass of wine won't hurt anything," he says. "We're celebrating."

She pours two glasses and assures us our waiter will be along soon. I pick up my glass and smile across the table at River.

"What should we toast to? How about to a successful new career?"

River grins back, picking up his glass as well. "To our future," he suggests instead, clinking his glass to mine.

"To the future," I repeat, lifting it to my lips for a sip.

We place our order once the waiter comes, and then River excitedly tells me about the contract he was offered. It's generous, and obviously the publisher has a lot of confidence in his graphic novel.

"I'm so proud of you," I tell him honestly.

"I couldn't have done it without you."

I wave him off. "All I did was set up a meeting, the rest of it was all you."

"You know it was more than that," he argues. "You encouraged me and inspired me. You're my muse."

I blush a little at that. "I always wanted to be someone's muse," I tease.

Our food comes, and we enjoy ourselves,

taking our time eating while we talk and flirt.

"I want you to know I meant it back at the house," River says once our dessert is delivered. "I'm all in with this, Easton."

I shove a forkful of tiramisu into my mouth, trying to hide the panic on my face. I want to tell him I'm all in too, but how can I say it when I know I'm still lying to him? I can't tell him the truth tonight when we're celebrating.

I search for words to say, at a loss for several seconds.

"I think it's time I clean out Paul's stuff from the extra bedroom," I blurt to my own surprise.

"If you think you're ready," River says, not seeming the least bit bothered by my slow pace at getting over my husband. It's one of a million things I love about him.

"I think it's time. It would be nice to have a room to work in again, and maybe..." I take another bite of the dessert.

"Maybe?" he prompts after a few moments.

"Well, if maybe one day you were to move in, it would be nice to have a place we could both work. You'll probably want to write a sequel or something once this graphic novel becomes a *New York Times* bestseller."

I can tell River gets stuck on the *move in* part because his smile gets so big it's almost blinding.

"Good thinking," he agrees casually, but the look in his eyes is anything but. "You know, you don't have to get rid of everything, you could put some things in storage."

"That's a good idea."

"I'll help if you want."

"I'd like that," I say. "We can start this week-end?" Maybe by then I'll have figured out a way to tell him the truth, because I can't put it off much longer. It's not fair to either of us.

CHAPTER 24

Easton

I hardly sleep on Friday night, tossing and turning, practicing the conversation in my head over and over again with every conceivable outcome—River feeling disgusted and betrayed, River understanding completely and promising he still loves me, River hauling off and punching me before storming out and never coming back.

"It's three in the morning," Fox answers the phone in a gruff voice. "Is this going to become a habit?"

"Sorry."

"It's fine, East. Tell me what's up."

"I'm going to tell him in the morning."

"Good," he grunts, still sounding half-asleep.

"What if he hates me once I tell him?" I ask.

"He might," Fox concedes, and my stomach drops.

"You're not supposed to say that. You're supposed to tell me he loves me, and no matter what, things will work out," I scold.

"I'm sorry, in the future could you send me my portion of the script ahead of time so I'm prepared?" he mocks and then yawns.

"I'm really scared," I confess. "I don't know what I'll do if I lose him."

"You'll still have me. We got through Paul's death, and we can get through this."

"Thank you."

"Anytime. You know that. Now, can I get back to sleep?"

"Yeah, sleep," I say. "I'll let you know how it goes tomorrow."

"Good luck."

We hang up, and I try to sleep a little longer before giving up and going out to the living room to work on my next graphic novel. The publisher was thrilled with the last one I turned in, as usual, and I wonder what they'll think when they get this one. I settle at my desk in the corner of the room and pick up my red colored pencil. I wonder what my fans will think. I smile to myself imagining the uproar in the fan chat rooms when they see I'm using color again.

I work until the sun starts to peek through the window, and then I drag myself away from my desk and into the shower so I can make myself human before River shows up. My stomach ties itself in complicated knots, my heart beating out a frantic rhythm. I'm too nervous to even have tea or breakfast before he shows up, my stomach protesting at the very thought.

River knocks on the door around nine, and he greets me with a sweet kiss and a bouquet of fresh flowers when I open it. The flowers are all shades of pink and yellow and orange, and I take them from him with a smile.

"They reminded me of the sunrise at the beach," he explains.

"They're beautiful."

I take them to the kitchen to put them in a vase, my brain stuck on repeat, going over the speech I prepared and spent all night practicing.

"You okay, baby?" River asks as I flutter aimlessly about the kitchen for a moment, opening and closing cabinets simply for something to do with my hands.

"Yeah, I didn't get much sleep last night."

Understanding dawns in his eyes and for a second, I wonder if somehow, he already knows what I need to tell him. Is it possible he's put the pieces together? He rounds the counter and loops his arms around my waist, leaning close and bumping his nose against mine.

"We don't have to do this today. If you're not ready to clean out the room, there's no rush."

I swallow hard and shake my head.

"It has to be today. I've put it off long enough already."

He kisses my cheek but takes his time in releasing me. "Okay, lead the way then."

I need to tell him the truth. I need to tell him now. But when I open my mouth, the words don't come out and I hate myself a little bit.

I have all day, I assure myself. It's going to be

today, no matter what.

We head into the second bedroom, into the sea of boxes, overflowing with Paul's things. And we get to work.

The morning goes by quickly. We start at the back of the room and put things into two piles —donate and storage. I'm proud of myself that the donate pile is significantly larger than the storage pile, which mostly consists of important mementos like Paul's wedding ring and ticket stubs from the first concert we went to together. But I still haven't worked up the courage to come clean. With lunchtime looming, I decide I need to get it over with, rip off the Band-Aid and just tell him already.

"I'm going to use the bathroom real quick," I tell River, excusing myself while he moves on to the next box.

I close and lock the door behind me, turning to the mirror to face myself. "You can do this," I tell my reflection. "He deserves to know. You love him, and he deserves to know."

I splash some water on my face and take a few deep breaths. It's time to tell the truth, and if he hates me after this, then it's no one's fault but my own.

When I get back from the bathroom, River is standing in the center of the room looking down at a card in his hands. It takes me several seconds to realize what it is, but as soon as I do, my heart stops.

"River?" I say his name through a dry throat, my heart beating double time now, my lungs feeling too tight.

He looks up slowly, his eyebrows scrunched together.

"I wrote this. How did you get this?"

"I can explain."

"Was…" His face goes pale, and he reaches up to put a hand over his heart. "Paul was my donor?"

A sob bursts from my throat, and I nod.

"How long have you known?"

"River, I…"

"How long?" he asks again, his voice sounding weak and broken.

"Before we met. I asked Fox to find you."

The silence hangs so heavy between us it's almost palpable.

"I have to go."

"River, wait," I beg, reaching for him as he brushes past me without stopping. The sound of the front door slamming echoes through the house seconds later like a gunshot.

"Fuck," I curse loudly as soon as he's gone, my heart feeling like it's shattering in my chest as my breath comes in short, ragged pants. I should've told him sooner, I know that.

River

I'm in a daze as the reality of the situation washes over me. I lean back and let my head fall against the headrest, my apartment building looming in front of me. I didn't think before storming out of Easton's place, *couldn't* think as I stood there holding the proof of his lies in my hand. But now I have questions. So many fucking questions.

Was this all just a way for him to hold on to his dead husband? Did he ever even love *me*?

My heart aches like it's been used as a punching bag, my throat burning as tears threaten to spill from my eyes.

No wonder Fox wanted me gone so badly. He was only trying to look out for me. He fucking knew, and he was watching the goddamn train wreck happen.

"Fuck!" I shout, slamming my fist into the steering wheel, a broken sob wrenching from my chest. Once it's free, I can't stop the rest that follow as I slump forward and let them wrack my body, tears spilling down my cheeks unrestrained.

I don't have a clue how long I sit in my car crying my heart out, but by the time I get myself under control, my eyes are puffy and swollen, and my throat feels raw. My entire body shakes as I reach for my phone, a bone deep exhaustion making me want to crawl into a dark hole and never come out. I feel betrayed on the deepest level and completely fucking heartbroken.

Brandon answers his phone on the third ring. "Hey, what's up? I thought you were with your man today?"

I open my mouth to answer and another sob

falls from my lips. Pathetic.

"Oh shit, River, what happened? Are you okay? Where are you?"

"I just got home. I—I'm not…"

"I'll be there in five minutes," he says before hanging up.

I manage to drag myself out of the car and up the stairs to my apartment. Every step I take feels like a herculean effort, but at least it takes me closer to my bed. When I get inside, I leave my door unlocked so I won't have to get up when Brandon gets here. Maybe I shouldn't have called him. I don't want to talk to him about what happened. I don't want to think about it. I want to go to sleep and wake up to realize this was all a horrible dream.

I kick off my shoes and crawl under the blankets, pulling them over my head. I feel like I could cry more, but I'm out of tears. That doesn't stop the occasional dry sob from breaking free from my chest.

Why did I think love was so great? Why did I dream of something and wish for something that could hurt me this badly? I'd have been better off never knowing what it could be like to feel like I'd found the other half of my soul just to have it ripped away in such a cruel way.

The sound of my front door opening sounds muffled and far away, and I tell myself I need to pull it together, so I don't embarrass myself in front of Brandon. Then I remember that he literally held a container for me to piss in at the hospital when I was too weak to do it myself, and maybe having him see me heartbroken isn't the worst he's seen me at.

My bed dips with Brandon's weight, and I push the covers off my face, but don't move other than that. I brace for him to ask what happened, but he doesn't. Instead, he puts a hand on my leg through the blankets and launches into a ridiculous story about a hookup gone wrong over the weekend that would likely have my laughing if my heart wasn't in a million pieces inside my chest.

"I'm hungry; how about I order a pizza?" he suggests, and I consider protesting, telling him I'd rather have something healthier, but right now a greasy, cheesy pizza sounds like heaven.

"Yeah, pizza sounds good," I agree, my voice rough and scratchy.

He orders the pizza, and I manage to push myself to a sitting position, running my hands over my face and through my hair.

"His husband was my heart donor," I say as soon as Brandon finishes ordering the pizza.

His mouth falls open, and his eyes go so wide that I actually find it in me to laugh at the goofy expression on his face. "Did he know?"

"Yup," I answer with an edge in my tone. "He knew before we even met. He tracked me down on purpose."

"Holy shit, that's fucked up. So, the whole relationship was, what? A fucked-up way of mourning his husband?"

I rebel against his words as soon as I hear them. Yes, I had the exact same thought when I was breaking down outside in the car, but I don't want to believe it. Could Easton really fake all of that? The way he kissed me so intensely? The lunches packed specially for me? The weekend at the beach, all wrapped up in each other? If it was all part of his plan to trick me into a relationship, why did he resist at first? He felt guilty about it; I know he did. He even tried to ghost me after the first time we went to the art fair. I was the one who sought *him* out again, who insisted on us being friends.

"I don't think so," I admit, and as soon as I say the words, one of the knots in my chest eases.

"What's the problem then?"

"He lied. He knew from the beginning, and he lied about it."

"Yeah, that's fucked up," he agrees. "But…" He pulls a sympathetic face, and I clench my teeth.

"But what? You think it's okay that he pretended not to know me? That every time his husband was brought up, he left out a vital piece of information that I had every right to know?"

"No, but…I mean, how do you tell someone that? Imagine having to explain that to someone you just met."

"Fine, it would've been weird when we met, but he could've told me later," I point out.

"When?" he asks. "When you were telling

him you were falling in love with him? When you were planning dates every weekend and whisking him off to the beach at a moment's notice? When you two were so damn happy and adorable it should've been illegal?"

"I don't know," I snap. "But he should've told me."

"Look, you have every right to be mad. You *should* be mad. But don't write this off without talking to him about it is all I'm saying. What you guys have is special, even a horndog like me can see that."

My stomach twists, and I snort a laugh.

"Take a day or two to be pissed, to lick your wounds and make him sweat, and then go talk to him about it."

"Okay," I agree.

"Good man." Brandon reaches over and pats me on the shoulder. "Now go wash your damn face so the pizza guy doesn't think I'm the one who just dumped you when he gets here."

CHAPTER 25

Easton

I pick up my phone to call River at least a dozen times over the next few days. I want to explain, but I doubt anything I have to say could make this situation better. Fox was right; I should've told him sooner. Or maybe I should've left him alone to begin with.

My heart protests at the thought, aching with loneliness at the thought of never having found River. He completes me just like Paul completed me, and even if I'd known the ending with Paul, that wouldn't have stopped me from loving him for a single second.

I spend time drawing, but instead of blacks and grays, I burn through just about every colored pencil I have. When I lost Paul, I went numb, retreating into myself for protection, shutting down and refusing to feel anything but loss. Now I feel too much of everything—anger at myself for the way I handled things, happiness for the way River shook me awake and forced me to live again, gut wrenching pain that he's gone...and on and on, the colors pour out of me like never before.

I draw everything—memories, feelings,

wishes, fears. And then I throw them away and draw more. It's therapy and torture all at once. I draw until my fingers cramp, and my back aches from hunching over my drawing table. I draw until a knock at the door finally makes me stop.

I'm expecting it to be Fox, somehow inherently sensing my inner turmoil like only he can do.

My breath catches when I pull open the door to find River standing there. He doesn't open his arms for a hug, and the smile I'm so used to seeing is absent from his face, but he's fucking *here,* and I'm so relieved my knees almost give out.

"River." His name feels like a prayer on my lips, and I notice a slight softening of his features for a second before he fixes his frown back in place.

"Can I come in?"

"Of course." I step back to make room for him to step inside, and he heads straight for the living room. Even from feet away, I can see his hands shaking before he shoves them into his pockets, shifting awkwardly as his eyes land on my mess of pages and colors littering my desk in the corner of the room.

"Therapy," I say as way of explanation, and River nods.

"You said you could explain," he says after a few seconds of strained silence. "So, explain."

I take a deep breath, hurrying to untangle my thoughts, painfully aware of the stakes of this conversation. Sinking down onto the couch, River follows me, claiming a seat as far from me as possible but angling his body in my direction, which gives me a small sliver of hope.

"I needed to know at first. I am *so* sorry. I kept trying to find the right time to tell you, and every day that went by it got harder. It's no excuse for what I did, and I can never tell you how truly sorry I am for hurting you." I'd throw myself at his feet to beg for his forgiveness if I thought it would help. "I wasn't planning on meeting you or getting to know you; I just had to know if..." I bite my lip, trying to find a nice way of phrasing it.

"If I was worthy?" he guesses, and I give a sharp nod.

"Yes." I wait to see his reaction, but his face remains passive, so I push on. "Fox told me you were a good guy and showed me a few pictures of you, and that was it. I was working through the grief, but I had no intention of doing anything else about it. Then, I saw you. I was walking home from dropping off a book to my agent, and I saw you on the street. My heart stopped. I swear I couldn't breathe, I couldn't think, all I could do was stare at you." I use the back of my hand to wipe away a stray tear before placing it back on my bouncing knee. I can't even look at River, but I can't keep from looking at him at the same time. I hate myself for hurting him, and I desperately need him.

"You saved me from stepping in front of a bus," he says as if he's only now remembering it.

"Yeah. And even then, I was going to leave it

at that. I didn't want to mess up your life or make you feel bad. Who wants to look into the face of the grieving spouse of their organ donor?"

The frown on River's lips deepens, and I fight the urge to kiss it away. He has a mouth made for smiling and kissing and laughing. Not frowning. Never frowning.

"I get it," he says. "*I* asked you to lunch. *I* pushed friendship even when you tried to blow me off. *I* was the one who pushed for even more."

"I'm glad you did," I admit. "I know I was reluctant, and I know I made some wrong decisions, but I don't regret what's happened between us for a second."

River's brow furrows, the lines on his forehead deepening. He hunches forward and rubs his hand over his mouth before looking back at me with so much sadness in his eyes it knocks the wind out of me.

"Did you ever really love me or was this always about Paul?" he asks. "I have to know. If I didn't have Paul's heart, if it was someone else's, would we still be together?"

"Oh, River." I can't take another second of the distance between us, so I inch toward him, bracing for a rebuff. He doesn't stop me, so I keep moving until I'm right next to him, able to feel the warmth of his body and count his breaths.

"I love your heart," I admit, putting a hand over the rough scar on his chest and feeling the steady beat that used to belong to Paul. "But I adore your soul too." I look into his eyes, feeling our connection through every fiber of my being. "I know this situation is crazy, and when I went in search of the person who got Paul's heart, all I wanted was to know a part of him was still alive out there somewhere. I didn't expect to find you, and I sure as hell didn't expect to fall for you, but I'm so glad I did. I love every single part of you, parts that used to be Paul, and all the parts that are utterly and truly *you*."

"What if the only reason I love *you* is because of Paul's heart?" He puts words to the fear I've had since he first told me he loved me, shaking my very foundation.

"*Is it* the only reason?" I ask, barely above a whisper.

"I don't know." He sounds plaintive when he answers, his eyes growing even more sad as they stay locked on mine. "For years after the transplant, I'd get in these moods where I would fucking *ache* with a loss I couldn't put a name too. I felt like I was missing a limb. It was like a bone deep loneliness that I sometimes wouldn't be able to shake for days. I haven't felt that since the day we met. I think...I think I missed you without even knowing you. I think *Paul's heart* missed you."

More tears stream down my cheeks. On some level, I like hearing that the only living part of Paul still found a way to love me, but it's not enough. As much as I love Paul, as much as I'll always love him, he's gone, and River is right here.

"Is that the only reason you wanted to be with me? Because I got rid of the loneliness you didn't understand?"

He seems to think it over for a few moments, his forehead scrunching and his legs bouncing as he chews his bottom lip. If the situation wasn't so serious, I might make a joke about him not hurting himself thinking so hard.

"I love your smile," he finally says. "I love your passion for the things you enjoy like your art and your garden and cooking. I love the way you feel in my arms when I hold you. I love the sweet notes you slip into my lunch. You make me feel better just being around you. You make *everything* better."

Relief rolls through me so acute I can't stop the laugh that bubbles past my lips, turning quickly to tears. Not sad tears or orgasm tears, happy tears.

"Maybe the initial connection you felt to me was because of the heart," I concede. "But I don't believe for a second that's what made you love me, River Williams. I think you're in love with me just like I'm in love with you—madly, wholly, and because we're the perfect fit."

His Adam's apple bobs as he swallows, hope blossoming in his eyes.

"I don't want to lose what we have," he says. "It hurt like hell when I found out, but I don't want this to be the end."

"Then it won't be the end," I agree, reaching

for his hand and linking my fingers through his. He lets me do it, squeezing my hand once we're connected. "I want a future with you. I want a life with you. I want everything."

Finally, a smile graces his beautiful lips. "You know I can't help but give you everything you ask for."

"Good." I smile too, leaning forward and pressing a kiss to his lips, sweet and claiming and full of promises. When I pull back, my mouth seems to have developed a mind of its own and I blurt, "We should get married."

River's eyes go wide, and I can already hear the reasonable excuses—we've only been together a few months, he *just* found out the truth and we should give it some time to sink in, we should try living together first. I brace for him to say any or all of those things.

"Okay," he says instead, and joy lights me up like fireworks.

"Okay?"

"Yes, let's get married."

I scramble into his lap and kiss him again until we're both breathless.

He wraps his arms around me and manages to stand, albeit a little wobbly in the execution. I laugh against his lips, the joy inside me bubbling up and spilling out. His chest rumbles in matching amusement, his grip on me tightening.

River manages to make it down the hallway to the bedroom and drops me on the bed unceremoniously, and just like that the spark is lit. I can't believe I almost lost him because of how stupid I was, because of my secrets. I grab the back of his neck and drag him into a kiss, deep and desperate and full of apology.

"I promise I'll never keep anything from you again," I murmur against his mouth, my hands groping with his clothes to get them off as quickly as possible. I need to feel him. I need to know that I didn't ruin things beyond repair.

"I love you so much, Easton," River whispers as he kisses his way down my neck, his fingers easily undoing the buttons on my jeans, now a virtual expert at it. "I can't wait to marry you and spend the rest of our lives together."

A sob falls from my lips, and I cling tighter to him. I didn't think I'd ever want a future with anyone but Paul, and now I can't imagine one without River.

"I need you," I gasp. "I need to feel you inside me." I lift my hips up so he can drag my jeans down my legs, the rough scrape of the denim against my skin waking up all of my nerve endings.

He groans in agreement, and our clothes quickly form a pile on the floor. I run my hands over his now bare chest, stopping when I reach his scar. River's breath catches, and our eyes meet. I can see uncertainty in his gaze as I lean forward and brush a kiss to the center of his scar before trailing my lips up his throat, over his chin, his lips, his eyelids, and finally placing a kiss in the middle of his forehead as well.

"Heart, mind, and soul, River, I promise."

A relieved sounding breath puffs past his lips, and his mouth seeks out mine, kissing me desperately as our achingly hard cocks grind against each other, hot and so fucking good. Each rock of his hips making me ache for more. My fingers dig into his shoulders, my legs wrapping around his as I meet him thrust for thrust.

When he pulls his mouth away from mine, I make a disgruntled noise, and he chuckles.

"Just need to grab the lube."

"Oh, in that case," I joke, letting him go so he can reach into the bedside table. His hand hesitates, and he turns his head to shoot me a wicked grin.

"One of these days I'm going to have to watch you use this vibrator, but right now I need to be inside you, so it'll have to wait."

My body flames at the idea of River watching me pleasure myself, whispering hot things into my ear as I fuck myself with my vibrator. My cock twitches, and I moan.

"Yes," I agree breathlessly.

He snatches the bottle of lube and rolls back toward me. He takes his time prepping me like he always does, seeming to take as much pleasure as I do having his fingers slowly, carefully fucking my ass until I'm a trembling, begging mess.

When his cock finally pushes into me, I sob with relief, wrapping my legs around his hips again and feeling every hard, throbbing inch as he enters me. By the time he's fully seated, my cock is leaking precum like a faucet, and my balls are heavy and tight. I clench around him just to feel him all the more intensely, and we both cry out.

He pulls back out slowly, nibbling at my collar bone and giving me chills as his cock drags against the bundle of nerves deep inside me.

Without warning, he rolls us over so I'm on top, his cock still buried deep inside me as I straddle his hips. He has a playful smile on his lips as he looks up at me, his hands on my waist.

"I want to watch you ride me."

I groan, putting my hands on his chest and using it for leverage as I lift myself off and then slam back down, making us both moan. From this position, he feels even bigger inside me, making me even more full. I lean back and do it again, feeling the entire length of his cock as it presses against my prostate and steals my breath. Leaning even farther back, I put my hands on his knees and let my head fall back on a deep moan, the full feeling so intense I start seeing stars.

"Fuck, that's good," I gasp, lifting myself up again and thrusting down, over and over. I'm tired of the slow, gentle fucking. We can save that for another day when I'm not out of my mind from having nearly lost River.

I fuck myself shamelessly on his cock, taking pleasure from every gasp and moan that falls from his lips. River wraps his hand around my cock, and my eyes roll back. He runs his thumb over my precum slicked, sensitive head while his other hand encircles the base of my cock and strokes me.

"Oh fuck, oh fuck," I moan, my balls constricting, my muscles tightening as tears leak from the corners of my eyes. "*Yesyesyesyes*," I chant as heat explodes from the pit of my stomach and races through my veins, my hot, sticky release pulsing out over River's fingers, my ass clenching and releasing around his cock.

River throws his head back and moans deep from his chest, and I can feel the answering pulses of his orgasm as he pumps inside me.

I lean forward and claim his lips as our orgasms taper off, leaving us breathless and sweaty. Our lips move lazily against each other, the lingering taste of our pleasure drawing content little sounds from both of us.

Eventually his softening cock slips out of me, and I roll off of him. River climbs out of bed and goes to the bathroom to clean himself up. I stretch happily, feeling my joints pop and my muscles twitch.

River returns from the bathroom and climbs back into bed, pulling me into his arms so I can rest my head on his chest. Our legs tangle together, and he runs his fingers gently through my hair like he loves to do so much.

"Will you tell me about him?" he asks after a few minutes of easy silence.

"Paul?" I ask.

"Yeah, I want to know more about him. I know how you met, but that's it. What was he like? What'd he do for a living?"

"He was the sweetest man I've ever met," I tell him. "He'd give a stranger the shirt off his back if he had it. That's how I knew..." I clear my throat and blink back tears as my fingers absently trace along his scar.

"How you knew he'd want to be an organ donor?" he guesses, and I nod. "How'd he die?"

"An accident on a job site. He worked in construction. He loved it so much, I swear I've never seen anyone happier to get up at the crack of dawn every day, no matter the weather, to go do manual labor all day."

"He sounds amazing; I wish I could've met him."

"Me too," I agree wistfully, glancing over at the picture of Paul and me on our wedding day, right on top of my nightstand. My heart gives a happy little squeeze at the thought of having a second photo right next to it of River and my wedding.

We lay in bed until the sun starts to set, and our stomachs start to growl, talking about Paul and the past, and more importantly, our future.

"I don't think I want a big wedding," I confess. "All I want is to pile into the car with Brandon and Fox and have the four of us drive up the coast to Massachusetts and get married on a beach outside a quaint little bed and breakfast."

River tilts my face up and presses a kiss to my lips and then the tip of my nose. "That sounds perfect. Let's go as soon as possible."

CHAPTER 26

River

"River, how are you?" My mom answers the phone.

"I'm good. I wanted to see what you're up to this weekend?" I ask, chewing my lip.

"Nothing. Did you want to come visit? I'd love to have you. Bring Easton, we can have a barbecue," she suggests excitedly.

"Actually." I blow out a breath, my heart hammering as I work up the courage to say this. "I wanted to see if you'd be willing to come with us to Cape Cod...for our wedding."

"Your what?" she sounds startled.

"Easton and I are getting married. It's a really small ceremony, just you, Brandon, and Easton's best friend, Fox." When I'd called Brandon to tell him, he'd been surprised at first by my one-eighty, going from likely breakup to elopement, but once I explained that we worked things out and how right this felt, he got on board fast. I have a feeling Fox was a different story. Easton was on the phone with him for over an hour, out on the back deck, making angry faces more than a few times, before he came back inside, kissed me on the cheek, and told me Fox would be there.

"Well, I know neither of you are pregnant," she jokes. "What's the rush?"

"It doesn't feel like a rush," I tell her. "It feels like I've been waiting for this my entire life. And I know that sounds dramatic, but it's the truth."

Before I called her, I considered whether or not to tell her the truth about Paul but decided that might be one too many things for this conversation. I'll tell her later, after the wedding.

She sighs. "I get it. That was how I felt about your father."

My breath catches. She hasn't talked about my dad since he died fourteen years ago. She never remarried, never even looked at another man as far as I know.

"Yeah?"

"I was absolutely smitten. If he would've asked me to elope the night we met, I probably would've," she admits with a giggle I've never heard from her before. "I could tell when the two of you were here a few weeks ago that it was the real deal. Some things are just meant to be."

"That means a lot. So, you'll come right?"

"Of course, I will. You think I'd miss my only son's wedding?"

I chuckle. "I was hoping not."

I give her the details of the B&B we booked and tell her about the small ceremony we have planned, and we chat a little longer before hanging up.

I toss my phone on the bed and pull my suitcase out from under the bed, opening it and setting it next to my phone. The scent of the beach still lingers inside, wafting to my nose and bringing memories of the sand between our toes, the crash of the ocean as background music as we made love for the first time. I smile to myself and then pick my phone back up to send a quick text.

River: I can't wait to marry you
Easton: Only four more days

My stomach flutters, and I start packing, tossing several days' worth of clothes into my suitcase, my medication, plenty of lube...we agreed to keep the wedding fairly casual, but I still place my favorite charcoal suit and teal tie into my suit bag to take along.

With everything packed, I head back over to Easton's place...soon to be my place too. The idea of waking up beside him every day for the rest of our lives leaves me nearly breathless. I never imagined I could actually love someone this wholly, want a life with someone this desperately.

I pull into his driveway, but I don't get out of the car right away. Instead, I sit there remembering our first kiss, my blurted confession that I wanted more than friendship from him. My heart beats a little faster, and I lift my hand to my chest to feel the beat against my palm. I think Easton was right, the initial connection, the draw

I felt toward him may have been in part due to Paul's heart. It's hard to deny how it fluttered the first time Easton touched me, how it practically jumped right out of my chest like it wanted to be closer to him. I don't think we fully understand everything about organ transplants, the cells and DNA still inside this heart belongs to Paul, and he loved Easton with everything he had. But I love him the same. It's not just my heart, Paul's heart, it's my mind and soul and every single cell in my body that feels a draw toward Easton, that wants to be around him and make him smile.

The front door opens, and Easton peeks his head out, giving me a curious look for sitting in my car for so long. He smiles and shakes his head, waving me inside.

I turn off the car and get out, striding across the lawn and sweeping Easton up into my arms. He gives a surprised squeak that turns into a muffled laugh against my lips. I can taste his joy as his tongue slips past my lips, and I make a vow to myself and to Paul that I'll spend the rest of my life bringing laughter and color to Easton's world in any way I possibly can.

"Let's get your stuff in my car; I want to get on the road right away," I say once I release him.

We decided we'd drive up tonight so we can get our marriage license first thing tomorrow, and then my mom, Brandon, and Fox will fly up for the weekend. I think my boss thought I was body snatched when I told him I was using *more* vacation time already. In the years I'd been with the company I'd only ever used the minimum required every year. I never had a reason to before.

CHAPTER 27

Easton

The first thing I see when I open my eyes on Saturday morning is River with a smile stretched across his lips.

"We're getting married today," he says as soon as he sees I'm awake.

"We are," I agree, mirroring his smile. "No cold feet?" I check.

River presses his feet against my shin and shakes his head. "Nope, toasty warm."

"Good." I lean in and steal a kiss, slipping my hands into his boxers and giving his ass a playful squeeze. "Want to join me for a shower?"

"Absolutely."

We kiss a few minutes longer before I manage to pull myself away from him and roll out of bed. He's right behind me, helpfully yanking down my underwear and running his hands over the curve of my ass when they fall to my feet. His hot lips trail along the back of my neck, and his half-hard cock presses against the small of my back.

"Mmm," I purr, pressing myself back into him. "And you say *I'm* the tempting one?"

"I'm not doing anything," he says, the feeling of his cock growing harder in complete contradiction to the innocence of his tone.

"Uh-huh."

"Come on, we'd better get moving. We promised everyone we'd meet them downstairs for breakfast."

"Ugh," I groan. "Why'd we invite anyone else to our wedding anyway?"

"Because they're family, and we love them," River points out.

"Right, that."

His chuckle vibrates from his lips to my skin, giving me goosebumps.

We manage to make it to the shower, stumbling inside mid-kiss once it's warm. Rivulets of hot water cascade over my skin, making us both slick as we grind against each other. I drag my mouth away from his and lap at his wet skin, drowning in the taste of him.

River reaches for a bar of soap and rubs it between his hands until it gets sudsy, and then he grips my hips and turns me around. I lean back against him, closing my eyes and letting my head fall on his shoulder as he runs his soapy hands all over me, not seeming to be in any hurry at all in spite of his insistence that we needed to get to breakfast.

When his hand wraps around my erection, I gasp and thrust into his fist as he nibbles at the back of my neck, his own stiff cock grinding demandingly against the curve of my ass.

"You're the most beautiful man I've ever seen," he murmurs near my ear, his other hand slipping into the crease of my ass so his soapy fingers can tease my hole. "You're brilliant and sweet and incredible," he continues to praise as the tip of his finger slips inside of me, drawing a shuddering moan from me, his grip on my cock tightening as he moves his hand faster.

My chest heaves, and River keeps up with his unending stream of words full of love and praise and awe, his finger pumping in and out of my hole as my cock throbs in in grasp. I whine and pant, tears mixing with shower water as they trickle down my face.

"Please, please, please," I chant, pressing back onto his finger and then thrusting into his hand over and over until I'm dizzy with desire and electricity is crackling up my spin.

"I love you so much," River whispers, his lips brushing the shell of my ear, his words sending me over the edge. My release coats his hand and is quickly washed away, down the shower drain. I rut into his hand, my hole pulsing around his finger until I'm spent and boneless, sagging against him.

As soon as I'm functional, I turn to face him, dropping to my knees and sucking him enthusiastically until his hot cum fills my throat and spills from my lips.

We finish our shower, washing up lazily, both high on orgasm endorphins and each other.

A giggle falls from my lips as we dry ourselves off, and I notice the way River's eyes light up at the sound.

By the time we manage to make it down to breakfast, Fox, Brandon, and River's mom are nearly finished eating.

"Look who finally decided to join us," Brandon says mockingly when we reach the table.

"We had to shower," River defends.

"Uh-huh, sure you did."

"Sit down, baby, I'll get your tea," River offers, brushing a kiss to my cheek and then making his way over to the coffee and tea station set up on the other side of the room. I smile after him, sinking down in my seat.

"You're as bad as he is with the heart eye thing going on," Brandon teases, and I shrug.

"I can tell how happy you make my son," his mom says, reaching over and putting a hand over mine.

Fox doesn't say anything, just gives me a tight smile.

We linger over breakfast for a while, River and I eating while the other three sip their coffee or tea and make small talk. Under the table I bump my foot against his, press our knees together, brush my fingers over his thigh, any excuse to touch him. It's not so different from the morning before Paul's and my wedding, the giddy feeling of love and possibilities, the excitement of the future laid out before us. Expect before my first wedding I was nervous as hell. I wondered if we were too young, if it really was possible to love one person forever, if Paul would eventually get sick of me, what it would be like to live with someone else for the rest of my life. Not that I don't have any doubts about how quickly River and I are moving, but I've learned the lesson well that tomorrow is never a guarantee.

After breakfast, River and I go our separate ways to get ready. My suit is already in Fox's room where I put it last night.

My hands tremble as I button up my dress shirt. I never thought I'd get married again, but every time I think about standing at the altar with River, a giddy feeling bubbles up inside me.

"You don't have to do this, you know," Fox says, handing me my tie. "You haven't been together long; what's the rush?" It's more or less the same thing he said on the phone when I told him the news, but I suppose he thinks it might be different face to face.

"Some best man you are. Is this the same speech you gave Paul before our wedding?" I tease, not letting his doubts penetrate my happy bubble, but Fox's face grows serious.

"I told him I'd never seen him happier, and I was glad he was sealing the deal before you came to your senses and bolted."

I stand up a little straighter, looking my old friend straight in the eye. "Don't I look happy?" I challenge. He studies me for a few seconds, reaching out to straighten my tie and then brushing the back of his hand against my cheek in an affectionate gesture.

"That you do," he concedes, a small smile finally forming on his previously scowling lips. "Guess we have a wedding to get to."

River

"You look so handsome," my mom says, brushing some lint off my shoulder and smiling at me.

"You look happy," Brandon adds. "I'll admit I was skeptical when you called and told me the news, but I can tell this is really what you want."

"It is," I agree. "I'm glad you're both here."

"I think it's time," Brandon says, checking his watch. "Are you ready for this?"

"Never been more ready for anything in my life." I grab the small bouquet of flowers I picked from the garden around the back, I checked with the owners first, and they tittered about how romantic I was. Actually, I had Brandon pick them so I wouldn't be rooting around in the dirt, but I pointed out which ones I wanted.

We step outside and find the officiant waiting just outside the gazebo we decided to have the ceremony in. I look around for Easton and find him coming out of another door with his arm looped through Fox's. They're both smiling, and when Fox looks up and notices me, he gives me a small nod that feels like all the approval I've been waiting for from him.

I meet Easton at the steps to the gazebo, and he lets go of Fox's arm to take mine.

"Are you ready?" I ask, and he smiles up at me.

"More than ready." I hold out the bouquet to him, and his eyes get a little misty as he reaches for the colorful arrangement of flowers. "They're beautiful."

"I promised you color," I remind him.

"That you did."

We climb the stairs to the gazebo, meeting the officiant right at the entrance, Brandon, my mom, and Fox standing on the steps behind us to watch.

While he starts with all the standard, *we're gathered here today* stuff, I only have eyes for Easton. His dimple is out in full display as he smiles at me.

"I understand you wrote your own vows?" the officiant asks, and we nod. "River, would you like to start?"

I take a deep breath and look into the deep, blue pools of Easton's eyes. "I always dreamed of the kind of love that could turn me inside out and make me feel like a whole new person; I just wasn't sure I'd ever find it. Then you came into my life, and I know you think I saved you, but you have no idea how much you saved me too. You saved me from myself in more ways than I could ever tell you. I promise to spend the rest of my life giving you color and beauty and love in all the ways I can think of. And I promise to love you with my whole heart, as well as my mind and soul," I vow, echoing the words Easton said to me.

A tear trickles down his cheek, and I reach over to wipe it away. He clears his throat and sniffles.

"Well, I can definitely promise you I'll find lots of reasons to cry all over you for the rest of our lives, since literally every emotion makes me do it," he jokes, and our family laughs behind us. "I wasn't living for a long time until we met. You brought me back to life, and you made me whole again. You're the most caring, loving, incredible man I know, and I can't believe I'm lucky enough to get to spend the rest of our lives together. I promise to always pack your lunch, complete with love notes," he says, and I let out a watery laugh. "I promise to always encourage and support you, and love you, heart, mind, and soul." As Easton finishes his vows, a blue butterfly flutters over and lands on his bouquet. His eyes widen as he watches it for a few seconds as it slowly fans its wings, enjoying the flowers, before taking off and floating away on the breeze.

I know it seems silly, but something inside me feels like it's Paul giving us his blessing, and the look in Easton's eyes tells me he thinks so too.

Another tear tumbles down his cheek, and I wipe it away again. We exchange our rings, and the officiant declares us married. I cup Easton's face between both my hands and kiss him soundly as our family hoots and cheers.

CHAPTER 28

Easton

After the ceremony, we walked to a bar just down the road to celebrate. I nurse a drink, not in the mood to get drunk, unlike our friends. River wraps an arm around me from behind, brushing his nose against the back of my neck and then pressing a kiss there.

"What can I do for you, husband?" I ask teasingly.

"Let's go back to the room," he whispers against my ear. "They won't miss us." He nods toward our family, drunk and dancing near the Jukebox.

"And what will we do back in the room?"

"I want you inside me." His lips brush my ear, and I shiver, his words sending a thrill through me. "Do you want that?" he asks. "I mean, do you like to do that?"

We hadn't discussed switching it up, falling into roles after our first time together. I was more than happy to bottom, and it was usually my preference, but I certainly wasn't opposed to topping every now and again. And the thought of having River underneath me, coming apart on my cock, was more than a little exciting.

"I like everything you want to give me," I answer, turning around in his arms and kissing him. "Let's go."

We don't bother to say goodbye; we'll see them in the morning, and I'm sure they won't begrudge us turning in early. We practically sprint back to the B&B and up to our room, closing the door behind us loudly.

Our lips find each other as our hands get busy with all the buttons and layers of clothes, shedding them as quickly as possible before climbing into bed, naked and hard. The cool metal of River's brand-new wedding band ghosts along my skin as he runs his hands over my stomach, and my nerve endings light up. I grab his hand and lift it to my lips, kissing each of his fingers and then the ring.

I was torn before the wedding about what to do about my other wedding ring, and River suggested I move it over to my right hand, so that's what I did.

"Roll over," I tell him, giving his ass a playful slap.

River flips onto his stomach, grabbing a pillow for his head, spreading his knees and tilting his hips so he's on full display for me.

"Oh my god, I have the hottest husband in the world," I groan, grabbing the globes of his ass in both hands and squeezing them, massaging them, parting them so his tight hole peeks out at me.

I lean close, pressing kisses on his ass cheek and then playfully biting. River gasps and laughs, squirming against the bed.

"The biting tickles," he complains with another laugh. I give him one more hard bite and he giggles, making me smile. I resume kissing instead, even if the sound of his laughter is one of my favorite sounds in the world. I trail my lips to the crease of his ass and then part it with my hands, dragging my tongue over his rough pucker.

"Oh wow," he moans, tilting his hips higher, begging for more. I lave my tongue down to his taint, over his balls, and then back up to his hole, teasing the rim until he relaxes enough to let me dip inside. I lick him open, loosening him with my tongue, savoring every gasp and moan that falls from his lips.

When I add a finger, he tenses, just the tip making his channel clamp down.

"Relax," I murmur, running my free hand up and down the back of his thigh to soothe him. "I promise if it hurts or you don't like it, I'll stop. Just take a deep breath and try to relax."

It takes a few seconds, but he finally eases up enough that I can return to licking him, slowly inching my finger inside until it's buried to the last knuckle, and he's shamelessly pushing back onto it, looking for more.

"Feels good?" I check.

"So fucking good," River groans into the pillow.

I nibble and suck his rim, crooking my finger in search of the little bundle of nerves inside him that will send him to the moon.

"Oh fuck," he gasps, and I smirk, *found it*. "Oh god, do that again," he begs, so I do. My tongue lighting up all the nerves around his hole, my finger presses against his prostate again, and he moans long and low.

"Hold on, I need lube." I carefully slip my finger out and reach into my suitcase beside the bed to grab what I need. I slick up my fingers and return to my place behind River. Using one hand to spread his cheeks again, I drag my lubed fingers over his hole, loving the way it twitches so greedily, waiting for me to fill it.

I slip two fingers inside this time, and he tenses again, but relaxes much faster than before, his fists balling on the pillow, his hips jerking as he groans.

He gets a taste of his own medicine as I take my time playing with his hole, fucking him with two fingers until sweat is beading on his back, and he's panting for me to give him more, and then I add a third and torture him a little longer.

When neither of us can take it any longer, I pour some lube onto my aching erection and replace my fingers with the head of my cock, pressing against his entrance. He moans again, spreading his legs wider as I grab his hips to pull them up for better leverage.

"Ready?" I check.

"Yes," he gasps. "Please."

I press inside him slowly, the heat of his channel engulfing me and making my eyes roll back in my head as heat licks at my spine. My entire body trembles with the restraint it takes to keep from slamming my entire length inside of him in one hard thrust.

When the front of my thighs are flush with the back of his, and I'm buried to the hilt inside him, I lean forward and press a kiss to the back of his shoulder, wrapping my arms around him and putting a hand over his chest to feel the frantic beating of his heart as he drags in ragged breaths.

"So full," he rasps out. "So good."

"Just wait, it gets even better," I promise, slowly pulling out until only the head of my cock is still grasped tightly by his channel, and then surging forward, filling him all over again. His moan echoes through the room, and I do it again and again. My lips never stop tasting his skin as I hump into him faster and faster, my balls bouncing against his and making my body tingle with pleasure and need.

It's too much and not enough all at once. I want it to go on forever, and I want to make him come right now. Good thing we have the rest of our lives to do this over and over and over.

I drag my hand from his chest, down his stomach where his muscles are coiled tightly, contracting with each breath he sucks in, and between his legs to grasp his cock.

"Easton," he groans my name, meeting my thrusts with his own, trying to take me deeper, harder. "Easton," he gasps again, and I feel his cock swell in my hand, growing stiffer, the veins feeling more prominent as his channel tightens around me. "I'm coming," he cries out, and so am I.

The pulsing of his hole milks my orgasm from me as his release coats my hand, running down my fingers and dripping onto the bed. I fuck him through it, chasing every shock of pleasure as I fill him with my cum.

I'm still inside him as he collapses forward, taking me with him. I stay on top of him, both of us breathing heavily until my cock starts to soften and slips out, leaving both of us sticky with sweat and cum.

River

Eventually I manage to get myself off the bed and cleaned up in the bathroom before slipping back under the covers beside Easton...*my husband*. I smile at the words, even just in my head. I run my hands through his curly hair, his head resting on my chest as we both bask in the afterglow of pleasure.

"I can't believe your butt is ticklish," he teases, pinching my ass cheek and making me squirm and laugh again.

"Oh, like you aren't ticklish at all?" I challenge, poking a finger into his side, searching for weak spots. When I reach his armpit, he tries to pull his arms in, wiggling away from me and giggling as I worm my way into tickle him.

"Stop," he gasps out between peals of laughter.

I relent, pressing a kiss to his lips and tucking him close to my side again.

"I love your laugh."

Easton puts his chin on my chest, looking up at me with his pretty blue eyes, his wild, brown curls falling over his forehead. "I love everything about you, River Harrison-Williams."

"Mmm." I kiss his lips again just because I can. "I like the sound of that."

"Me too," he agrees. We fall quiet for a few minutes basking in the peace of our synchronized breathing, his chest rising and falling against my side as he rests his head on my pec. "Do you want to move?"

"No way, I'm too comfortable."

He laughs again, and the sound burrows into my heart to make a home there. "No, I meant houses. Obviously, you're going to get out of your lease, and we'll live together, but should we sell my house and buy one together?"

"I love your house. It has your garden."

"I could plant another garden," he reasons. "I just don't want you to feel like I'm trying to fit you into Paul's and my life. I want to build a life with *you*."

"As long as we're in this together, I couldn't

care less where we live. I like your house, I'd be happy to live there. And, if in a few years we decide we want to move, we can do that too. But I don't want you to do anything because you think you're supposed to. I don't mind you having Paul's things, Hell, I have his heart," I joke, and Easton snorts a laugh.

"That's fair. I may have pictures but at least I didn't save any organs."

He traces a finger lazily up and down the center of my chest, over the scar and then down to my belly button.

"I want everything with you, Easton. I want shared space and stupid fights and maybe kids one day if we decide it's what we both want. I want a life with you, and I can't wait to find out what shape that takes."

"Me too." He turns his head and presses a kiss against my chest. "I want all of that, and a whole lot of this too." He gives me a wicked grin and cups my soft cock.

"Lucky for both of us we have all the time in the world."

"That we do," he agrees. "And I don't want to waste a minute of it."

We spend the rest of the night wrapped up in each other, and when it comes time to check out in the morning, we decide this is another place we'll have to add to our list to re-visit. Easton links his hand through mine as we walk to the car. I meant what I told him last night: I can't wait to see what our future looks like, no matter the shape it takes. But I'm pretty damn happy with our present too. I make a silent promise to myself that I won't take a minute of our lives together for granted. I'll remind him every single day how insanely in love with him I am. Forever.

EPILOGUE

Easton

The sound of birds chirping is the first thing that pulls me from a pleasant dream I was having about my husband. I stretch and groan as my joints pop, and my muscles twitch after being immobile too long. Reaching for River's side of the bed, I find it empty but still warm, the blankets messy.

"Good morning," he says, drawing my attention to the doorway where he's standing with a tray in his hands, gloriously naked. More than two years and I still can't get enough of him, and the way his eyes are devouring me as I push the blankets back so he can see exactly how much I'm appreciating the view lets me know he feels the same way.

"Behave," he chides, humor shining in his eyes. "I brought you breakfast in bed."

"What if I want a protein shake instead?" I tease, waggling my eyebrows at him.

"You're impossible," he says, setting the tray down on the nightstand on my side of the bed, right next to my two framed photos—one from each of my weddings, the two best days of my entire life.

I tilt my face up and smile sweetly at River. "Thank you for breakfast; it smells amazing."

He smirks and leans down to press a kiss to my lips, slow as molasses and just as sweet. I drag my fingers up his arm, feeling goosebumps form in my wake as the kiss deepens. I try to tug River into bed, and he chuckles against my lips but remains unmoving.

"Breakfast first," he says, pulling away and picking the tray back up.

As much as I wouldn't mind letting breakfast get cold, it makes me all gooey inside that he got up early to make it for me, so I pull the blanket back over my lap and sit up. He sets the tray on my lap and brushes another kiss to my cheek.

"Happy anniversary, baby," he murmurs against my skin.

I turn my head and claim his lips for a second time, careful not to spill the food and coffee.

"Happy anniversary. Two years is just the beginning of our life together."

"It is," he agrees.

Sometimes it's still hard to believe how far we've come and how much River has changed my life. River's graphic novel sold like crazy, including a studio optioning the film rights. So now we spend our days working at our separate drafting desks in our shared office space and still make time on the weekends to teach art classes at the community center and hit up the art fair down by the Riverwalk. And when my garden needs tending, River is always there with a shovel and a smile to help in any way he can.

I take River's face between my hands and kiss him soundly one last time, simply because I can.

"I love you more than anything, and I always will. Heart, mind, and soul." I whisper against his lips, just like I do every morning, because if there's one thing I learned from Paul, it's not to take any day for granted.

"I love you too. Heart, mind, and soul," River says back, like he always does.

The End

MESSAGE FROM THE AUTHOR

I want to say a huge thank you for taking this journey with me through Easton and River's epic love. This story truly came straight from my heart and I hope you loved it as much as I did. Before you ask, yes I do expect Fox and Brandon will get a story at some point. I didn't orignally plan it, but my characters do tend to have a habit of surprising me like that.

MORE BY
K.M.NEUHOLD

The Heathens Ink Series

➢ Rescue Me (Heathens Ink, 1). To read this story about dealing with PTSD and addiction, and finding true love during an inconvenient time: click here

➢ Going Commando (Heathens Ink,2). If you're looking for a lower angst story, you'll want to check out this sexy, fun friends-to-lovers with an epic twist! Get it Here

➢ From Ashes (Heathens Ink, 3). Don't miss this story about love in the face of deep physical and emotional scars: Click Here

➢ Shattered Pieces (Heathens Ink, 4). Grab this beautiful story about a feisty man who loves to wear lace and makeup trying his damndest to help a wounded soul heal: Click Here

➢ Inked in Vegas (Heathens Ink, 5) Join the whole crew for some fun in Las Vegas! Click HERE

➢ Flash Me (Heathens Ink, 6) Liam finally gets his men! Click HERE

The Heathens Ink Spin-off Series: Inked

➢ Unraveled (Inked, 1) And don't forget to read the sexy, kinky friends to lovers tale! Click Here

➢ Uncomplicated (Inked, 2) Beau, the flirty bartender finally gets his HEA! Click Here

Replay Series

➢ If you missed the FREE prequel to the Replay series, get to know the rest of the band better! Click Here

➢ Face the Music (Replay, 1): click Here

➢ Play it by Ear (Replay, 2): click Here

➢ Beat of Their Own Drum (Replay, 3): Click Here

Ballsy Boys

Love porn stars? Check out the epic collaboration between K.M. and Nora Phoenix! Get a free prequel to their brand new series, and the first two books now!

➢ Ballsy (A Ballsy Boys Prequel). Meet the men who work at the hottest gay porn studio in L.A. in this FREE prequel! Click Here

➢ Rebel (Ballsy Boys, 1) If anyone can keep it casual it's a porn star and a break-up artist. Right?? Click Here

➢ Tank (Ballsy Boys, 2) Don't miss this enemies to lovers romance that will set your Kindle on fire! Click Here

➢ Heart (Ballsy Boys, 3) Like a little ménage action with your porn stars? Don't miss bad boy porn star Heart falling for not only his nerdy best friend, Mason, but also his own parole officer, Lucky! Click

Here

➢   Campy (Ballsy Boys, 4) a sexy cowboy and a porn star with secrets! Grab Campy's story now! Click Here

ABOUT THE AUTHOR

Author K.M.Neuhold is a complete romance junkie, a total sap in every way. She started her journey as an author in new adult, MF romance, but after a chance reading of an MM book she was completely hooked on everything about lovely- and sometimes damaged- men finding their Happily Ever After together. She has a strong passion for writing characters with a lot of heart and soul, and a bit of humor as well. And she fully admits that her OCD tendencies of making sure every side character has a full backstory will likely always lead to every book having a spin-off or series. When she's not writing she's a lion tamer, an astronaut, and a superhero…just kidding, she's likely watching Netflix and snuggling with her husky while her amazing husband brings her coffee.